## BOOK NEWS

Sign up for exclusive updates and offers at news.jljarvis.com

# GET THE AUDIOBOOK

*jljarvis.com/ph2-evelyn*

# EVELYN'S PINE HARBOR AUTUMN

# EVELYN'S PINE HARBOR AUTUMN

PINE HARBOR ROMANCE BOOK 2

J.L. JARVIS

EVELYN'S PINE HARBOR AUTUMN
Pine Harbor Romance Book 2





Published by Bookbinder Press
bookbinderpress.com

ISBN (ebook) 978-1-942767-38-1
ISBN (paperback) 978-1-942767-37-4
ISBN (audiobook) 978-1-942767-56-5

# CHAPTER ONE

Eve leaned back and shut her eyes. "My first pumpkin spice coffee of the season."

While her daughter, Lydia, unpacked a bag of sandwiches, Allie closed the door to her shop and joined them in the back room for lunch.

"Mom." Lydia brushed her upper lip with her fingertips. "Whipped cream mustache? Not your best look."

Eve grabbed a napkin. "Oops."

Allie laughed. "No one's judging here."

Eve glanced at her daughter and raised an eyebrow. "Almost no one." She turned back to Allie. "It's a small price to pay for my favorite drink of my favorite season."

Lydia rolled her eyes. "You say that every year, and then Christmas comes along, and you're like, 'Autumn who?'"

Eve wrinkled her nose. "Maybe, but I do think autumn is highly underrated—hot mulled cider by a wood fire, warm apple crisp à la mode, and the feeling of change in the air as cool breezes toss crisp colored leaves."

Allie tilted her head. "You know, two of those three involved food."

Eve said, "If I could figure out a way to combine food with leaves, I'd make it three out of three. Speaking of food..."

The conversation took a turn toward their lunch preparations, which involved unwrapping sandwiches from the nearby deli. Wednesday lunches had become a tradition for Eve and Allie, who worked and lived next door to each other. Since starting work at Allie's shop, The Gallery, Lydia had been in school during Wednesday lunchtime and unable to attend. But now, with her high school graduation almost two months in the past, she was not only a regular but had also been awarded the dubious honor of fetching the food.

The conversation hit a lull while they dove into their sandwiches. Between bites, Lydia said, "If I'd known this was what lunch could be like, I'd have graduated early—or quit."

Allie set down her sandwich. "Tomorrow's the big day, isn't it?"

Lydia smiled nervously. "Yes."

Eve's eyes softened as she gazed at her daughter. "College. I can't believe it."

Lydia gave her mother a playful smirk. "Dry your eyes, Mom. It's not like I'm going away." She looked at Allie. "The community college is—what? Maybe four miles away?"

"Four and a half," Eve protested. "And my eyes *are* dry."

Lydia grinned. "Yeah, but you know you want to get just a little bit misty."

She was right, but Eve wouldn't admit it. If she got a little emotional, she was entitled to it. She had raised Lydia on her own, which had been no small feat. There had been some tough years along the way, but they'd made it. "All I want is to watch you follow your dreams."

Lydia rolled her eyes and turned to Allie. "See? She's been like this for days. But she's right. I do have big dreams—like making it through my first day of college without saying or doing something stupid. I have this recurring scene in my head of tripping over the classroom threshold and face-planting myself at the foot of the whiteboard. I just hope I don't break my nose on the marker ledge... all that blood smeared on the whiteboard."

Allie said, "You'll be fine."

Lydia's lips spread wide in a nervous semi-smile, showing her teeth.

"So... you're commuting. Are you taking your mom's car?"

She averted her eyes and said nonchalantly, "No, I've got a ride."

Allie crumpled her sandwich's paper wrapping and got up to throw it away. "That's nice. So you know someone else who's going to school there?"

Eve lifted her eyebrows. "You know him too."

Lydia got up to throw away her trash but not before shooting her mother a look.

Allie looked curiously from one to the other. "Well? Who?"

Eve looked to her daughter for permission, but all she got from Lydia was an eye roll, which Eve took to mean no.

Lydia exhaled. "It's Marco."

Allie looked pleasantly surprised. "Marco Silva?" Eve knew Allie's lingering smile would make Lydia uneasy enough, but Allie's words made it even worse. "Well, good. You two are so cute together."

Lydia looked horrified. "It's a ride. From my *friend*. There's no cuteness involved."

Allie glanced at Eve, who just bit her lips and shook her head slowly.

Lydia added, "And please don't mention it to Theo." It was a reasonable request, given the fact that Theo was not only Allie's boyfriend but also Marco's brother.

Allie nodded. "Not a word. Promise. But why would I? Like you said, it's only a ride."

*From a friend.* Eve was proud of herself for staying quiet.

Lydia furrowed her eyebrows. "Exactly." She headed for the door to the shop. "I'll go open The Gallery." She closed the door behind her.

Eve tossed her lunch wrapper and picked up her purse. "You know, sometimes I hear myself talk, and I can't believe what I sound like."

Allie folded her arms. "Which is what?"

Eve exhaled. "A mom."

Allie's eye sparkled. "You've earned the right."

Eve leaned closer and spoke quietly. "It's this thing with Marco."

Allie's eyebrows drew together. "Thing? You mean friendship?"

"Right. Don't get me wrong. Theo's raised him well. Marco's very likable. I guess that's my problem. He's too darn handsome and charming for anyone's good, let alone my daughter. I don't want Lydia to end up..." She didn't need to finish the sentence. Allie knew Eve's whole story. The fear had been fixed in Eve's mind for years. "Pregnant at seventeen, dreams dashed to the rocks. I just want to spare her a difficult life."

Allie exhaled, understanding. "I get that, but I think Lydia does too. She's seen how hard you've worked. She respects that."

"Really?" That was good to hear. She knew Lydia loved her, but whether she liked her wasn't always so clear.

"I'm not a mom," Allie said, "so I don't know exactly how you're feeling, but I've worked with Lydia for months now. She's a smart girl, and I trust her. I think you can too."

Eve sighed. "I know—at least my head knows. My churning stomach isn't quite so sure."

Allie gave her a hug. "You've made it this far."

She held Eve's shoulders and gave her a confident look. "You'll be fine. She will too."

Looking more terrified than convinced, Eve said, "Right," and left for work at the real estate office next door.

Eve barely noticed the bright morning sun streaming in through the window as she set down her coffee and knocked on Lydia's bedroom door. "The sink's leaking again. I had to shut the water off."

The door swung open. "It's my first day of classes, and I can't even shower?"

"I'm sorry, honey."

Lydia exhaled loudly. "If I don't wash my hair, I'll look like an olive oil dispenser—extra virgin."

Eve fought back a smile. "Do they even make olive oil dispensers?"

Lydia narrowed her eyes and pouted. "They won't have to now. I'll just wring out my hair."

While Eve grabbed her phone and shoved it into her purse, she said, "You can use the sink in the office break room downstairs to shampoo, then bring a bucket upstairs for a sponge bath."

Lydia wrinkled her face. "Great." But she headed for the bathroom to retrieve her shampoo. "What if people walk in?"

"I'll close the door to the back room, and I'll be at my desk standing guard—sitting guard, actually.

You'll be fine." While they both headed downstairs, Eve continued. "Caroline's out for the morning, showing houses to a couple. The only one else I'm expecting is the plumber—if I'm lucky. I just left a message on his voicemail."

"Mr. Vaughan, the soccer coach?"

"Probably not anymore. You haven't played soccer since you were..."

"Eight."

"Right. I doubt he's still coaching." Eve headed to the break room and began making coffee. "You know, he was my coach too. That would make him..."

"Old." Clutching her shampoo and conditioner, Lydia waited impatiently while Eve filled the coffee pot with water. "I'd love to hear more about your childhood soccer career, but I can't be late on the first day."

By the time the coffee was ready, Lydia was wrapping her head with a towel. A horn honked from the street.

"Oh, crap."

Eve set down her cup and shooed Lydia upstairs as she went to the real estate office door and unlocked it. She called out, "She's on her way, Marco!"

Marco Silva rolled down the window of his weathered SUV. "That's okay. I'm a few minutes early."

"Would you like some coffee?"

Grinning, he lifted a to-go cup.

Eve waved then stepped out of the way just in time for Lydia to rush past with wet hair hanging in loose brown clumps. "Love you! Bye!"

"Have a good day!" Eve exhaled as the SUV pulled onto the road. *This was not how this day was supposed to begin.* Retrieving her coffee, she sat at her desk to enjoy a moment of peace while it lasted.

The Welch's Real Estate office was housed in a century-old building. Caroline Welch, Eve's boss, had replaced the electrical wiring a year earlier. Now the plumbing was acting up. It was inconvenient, but she couldn't complain. Caroline was not only her boss. They'd also become close friends. When Eve had gone through a tough patch financially, Caroline had rented her the apartment upstairs for a fraction of its market value. She'd made it sound like Eve would be doing her a favor. Eve knew better, but she couldn't afford to turn down the offer. She and Lydia had a home and a true friend.

Eve had barely opened the email app when a knock sounded on the back door. Eve swung open the door and looked up. "Oh!"

Dylan Vaughan was a half foot taller than his father, with broader shoulders and slightly oversized facial features that gave a more rugged impression than his quiet manner delivered. His eyebrows drew together. "Didn't you call for a plumber?"

Eve realized her mouth was still open, so she

closed it. He waited while she came to her senses and said, "I was expecting your father."

"Will I do? I'm licensed."

She brushed her hair back. "Yes, sorry. Of course." She invited him in.

Dylan didn't smile, but he had the same amiable manner he'd always had. "Dad's retiring, and I'm taking over the business."

"Oh, well that's good... for him. And for you."

"Yeah, he's slowing down, but he won't admit it." His eyes twinkled. "My mom's not afraid to remind him, though. She's finally convinced him to buy an RV and travel the country." For the first time, Dylan smiled, and his eyes sparkled. "I give them a month—maybe two."

Eve smiled and began to relax. "Well, he deserves it. He's worked hard all his life." She raised her eyes to meet his then wished she hadn't. Emotions she'd thought were left in the past rose like a flash flood.

"So have you." He looked straight at her, just as he used to. He'd always seemed to see through her façade to the real Eve—the one who, after all these years, was still unsure of herself. She used to hate that look. She didn't like it all that much now, either. She wasn't even sure what he had meant. *So have you?*

Her expression must have revealed her reaction, because Dylan added, "I mean you've worked hard. You've been a great mom to your daughter."

A rush of emotion overwhelmed her. She

glanced down. Her eyes couldn't seem to settle. "Lydia."

"Yeah, I know. Dad keeps me posted. Not in a weird way—just in a Dad way—about everyone, not just you." He grinned, but it quickly faded as he looked away. "So, you've got a leak?"

That brought her back to solid ground. "Yes." She felt almost lucid again and even managed to smile. "It's the kitchen sink. Owen has fixed it before, but he warned us it would act up again. This morning, I woke up and came into the kitchen to make coffee and discovered I was standing in a puddle in front of the sink."

He smiled. "Let's take a look."

## CHAPTER TWO

Marco leaned across the car seat and pushed open the door. "Morning."

With an impatient sigh, Lydia plopped down in the seat. "What time is it?"

Marco furrowed his eyebrows. "We're fine." He looked back at the road and pulled into traffic, which for Pine Harbor, meant the half dozen cars driving through town at the moment. It was as close to a rush hour as Pine Harbor had.

Lydia rummaged through her backpack. When it went on for over a minute, Marco said, "What's wrong? Did you lose your freshly sharpened number-two pencils?"

Lydia dropped her hands on her still-open backpack and gave him a look that made him wish he hadn't asked. Maybe pens would have prompted a better response.

Something rolled out of her backpack and fell on the floor. "There it is!"

"What?"

"Lip balm."

*All that for that?* Suppressing a smile, Marco kept his eyes straight ahead, turning his head only if he absolutely had to do so for the sake of safe driving.

She glared suspiciously. "What?"

His eyes widened. "I didn't say anything."

Her expression fell into almost-instant sadness. "What?"

Marco was confused—worse. If he hadn't been driving, he would have left the room—or maybe the town. "You're not exactly a morning person, are you?" She inhaled with such purpose that he hastened to add, "It's fine! It's just good to know how it's going to be every morning, so I can..." *Wear a helmet,* he thought to himself but finished with, "Not bother you with... talking." With some effort, he maintained a neutral expression. Her frustration amused him, mainly because it was such a stark contrast to her usual air of quiet competence. But he wouldn't risk her wrath by even hinting at a smile.

When a traffic light turned red, he stopped and studied her. Her eyes were wide open. *Now what?*

"I'm sorry!" She winced.

"For what?" Accepting her apology seemed like a good enough option, but he had second thoughts, worrying that doing so would imply that she owed it to him. *This is just too darn confusing.* He'd always prided himself on being able to read people.

His brother called it his way with the ladies, but it wasn't just that. He liked women, and he liked making them happy—sometimes too happy. But Lydia was too hard to read—impossible, really. He was never quite sure where he stood.

Her shoulders sank. "It's my mom."

The light changed, and Dylan drove on. "What's wrong? Is she sick?"

"No, she never gets sick. It's just... mom stuff. Never mind." She clutched her backpack to her chest then looked up and blew air through her lips. "And I'm nervous." When he gave her a questioning look, she added, "About school."

"What? That's crazy."

"Yeah? Well, that's me."

Dylan just shook his head and pulled into the campus entrance. The lot was full, so he drove around, looking for a space to park, while Lydia looked at her watch. "Where's your first class?"

She looked as though she were in the middle of a tornado instead of a college campus. "The Humanities Building."

"Which is...?"

She pointed.

Dylan drove to the entrance. "Where's your last class, and when is it over?"

"Old Main, two fifteen."

"I'll meet you there."

She looked stunned, as though she couldn't accept the favor of curbside ride service.

They still had a few minutes to spare, but he

knew she would feel better if she got there early, so he pulled up to the entrance and stopped. He glanced toward the building. "Better go."

She looked surprised, which made no sense to Marco, but that was Lydia—bewildering, some might even say weird, but in a good way. Usually. Maybe not this morning, exactly.

"Okay. See you later." She hopped out of his car and walked briskly toward the building.

He watched her walk down the sidewalk then looked at his watch.

*Yeah, she'll be fine, but I'd better find a parking spot soon, or I'll be late.*

"WHAT IS THE MATTER WITH ME?" Lydia pondered it all the way to class. *I'm nervous, that's all.* Starting school was an exciting and stressful event for her. It always had been. "There's no need to be nervous," her mother used to tell her. Lydia was probably the only child ever whose mother told her not to worry so much about grades. But she did. She couldn't help herself. And then there was her shyness.

She had managed to hide her idiosyncrasies from others, except for her mother. Until now. All she had to do was ride in Marco's car and get dropped off for class. But in that short time, she had managed to dump her perfectionist-driven anxieties all over Marco. And he didn't deserve it.

On the other hand, if they were going to be friends, she supposed this was a good start. He'd just gotten a full dose of the real Lydia. Always the overachiever, she had just overachieved being grouchy at Marco, the guy who had offered to drive her to college every day. Every day. And he refused to take any gas money from her. So instead, she'd paid him back by being cranky. At this rate, she might find herself looking for new transportation.

Setting aside her regrets, she walked into class. After a quick scan of the empty seats, she selected the optimal seat for invisible Lydia. Studies showed that professors tended to call on students on their right side. Of course, that assumed they were right-handed. Left-handed teachers threw everything off. It wasn't that she didn't love learning. She just didn't like being called on. So she selected a seat on the professor's left, about halfway up in the invisible zone, where she hoped to spend a semester in obscure bliss, learning without being unduly troubled by excessive anxiety.

While Dylan followed Eve upstairs to the apartment, she wondered, *Does this make my butt look big? Why do I care? Because seeing Dylan brings back too many memories of a time I would rather forget.*

She couldn't think of that now. The only way she was going to get through this was to keep her mind focused on the matter at hand. As they arrived in the kitchen, she told him, "It leaks under the sink and pools on the floor."

"Okay. Let's take a look." He got down on his knees and stuck his head inside the cabinet while he searched with a flashlight.

While Eve watched and waited, her mind wandered, along with her gaze. *Hmm. Those glutes are no accident. Someone's kept in shape. Hiking? Good guess with those thighs. Maybe cycling. Or he could be a runner, but they're usually thinner. He sure didn't look that sinewy in high school. No... the eighteen years since then have been good to him.* Without thinking, she put her palm on her abdomen. *A few stomach crunches over the years wouldn't have killed me.* She'd kept her weight fairly in check, but her abs were a little too squishy.

Dylan popped out from under the sink. "I can get you fixed up for now, but those pipes are old. To be honest, anything I do to fix them is temporary. They need to be replaced."

"Owen said that the last time."

"Not surprising. Has my dad tested your water? Those old pipes can leach lead."

"I think he mentioned it once, but we might have gotten sidetracked. When Caroline bought the building, she installed water dispensers in the office and up here. We use those for drinking and cooking."

He glanced at the dispenser. "That's good.

People don't think enough about water quality, but it's serious stuff."

"Yeah, I guess I should have looked into it."

"I'll take a sample for testing. I've got a kit in the truck."

It sounded like a good idea, so she didn't object. But Eve had expected that to come more in the form of a question, especially from Dylan. He'd always seemed too mild-mannered to make a decision without asking first. But as she thought back on those high school days, she wondered how much she'd ever known Dylan. In spite of all that had happened, she knew little about him.

Doing a surprisingly good impression of Arnold Schwarzenegger, he said, "I'll be back."

"Okay, plumbinator."

He grinned then headed downstairs to the truck. She'd forgotten what a nice smile he had. Or maybe she'd never noticed. It was like having the sun come out and warm everything in its path. Those smile lines extending from his eyes were new. But overall, thirty-five was a good look for him.

In the midst of her musings, she realized he wouldn't need her standing guard over him while he worked, so she headed downstairs, where her own work waited. As she reached the last step, he rounded the corner and almost collided with her.

Grasping her shoulder to keep her from losing her balance, he said, "Sorry."

"No, it was my fault." Their eyes locked for a

second. It couldn't have been very long, but it was enough to send an electric charge through her. Still fixed on his gaze, she said softly, "I was just going to work."

He stepped back and gave her more room than she needed, as if there were a force field between them.

She could scarcely look at him. "I'll be down here in the office if you need me." *If you need me?* She walked away with wide eyes, blowing air through her lips. *Close call. I nearly had man contact.*

Eve sat at her desk, unable to work. This was why Dylan's father handled Eve's plumbing calls. Not that she'd ever asked him or that there were many calls. But Owen just knew. How could he not? Or maybe it had been Dylan who wanted to avoid her. In either case, it had been for the best.

Heavy footsteps descended the stairs, and Eve looked up.

"You're okay for now."

"For now?"

"Those pipes must date back to the Roman aqueducts."

Eve laughed. "Oh no. That bad?"

Dylan nodded. "While I was working, the pipe practically crumbled in my hands. I've patched it up, but it's only a matter of time before something else bursts."

"I'll tell Caroline. She's the owner. I just rent."

"Right. Well, have her give me a call."

"Will do."

"Tell her not to wait too long."

"Okay, thanks." She got lost in his gaze. Flashes of history, moments she'd buried, came to mind with harsh clarity. How many unspoken words and unexpressed thoughts still hovered between them?

His expression was gentle and wistful. "It's good to see you, Eve."

"You, too, Dylan."

LYDIA WALKED out of her last class, feeling elated. The day had gone well. She didn't hate her professors. In fact, she liked most of them so far. And the work seemed manageable. She could do this. She couldn't wait to tell Marco.

*Oh, Marco.* She remembered the morning. Oh well, she would apologize, and he would—fingers crossed—forgive her. Holding a grudge wasn't really his style.

She arrived at the end of the sidewalk and waited. At some point, she thought he'd mentioned that his classes got out an hour earlier than hers. Had she misunderstood? People walked by. Cars drove by. Minutes ticked by.

And then, there he was—fifteen minutes late, but still there. She smiled and headed for the passenger side, by which time Marco had slid down the passenger window and leaned around the girl in Lydia's seat. Well, it wasn't *her* seat, exactly, but it was where she'd expected to sit.

"Hi, Lydia!" he called out. "Hop into the back."

"Okay." *Did that sound cheerful? I hope I was cheerful. I tried.*

"I told—"

Lydia only heard something that started with J. *Jennifer? Jessica? Juniper?*

"—that I'd give her a ride to her car because her new heels gave her a blister."

Lydia missed her cue to make a sympathetic sound, but she managed a pleasant, "No problem."

*Blister, my foot.* Jennifer/Jessica/Juniper obviously liked Marco. Why wouldn't she? Marco was tall, with dark hair and dark eyes, strong shoulders, and a great butt—not that Lydia had ever admired him while he carried a case of booze to the bar and bent down, using his knees, which was the proper way to do it, unavoidably highlighting his glute definition. No, she'd never watched any of that. Clearly, Jennifer/Jessica/Juniper had taken note, and she liked him. *How nice for her.*

Fortunately, Lydia was doing a spectacular job of transitioning Marco from starry-eyed crush to a friend—her friend—her fist-to-shoulder, good old car-pool pal. So being displaced by a high-heeled girl—*Come on! Who wears heels to class?*—was fine. Just fine.

Lydia stared out the window and longed for an evening on her bed crocheting and reading a textbook. A few minutes later, Jennifer/Jessica/Juniper interrupted her daydream by talking, which really wasn't her forte. "Nice to meet you!"

"You too." *Smile, Lydia. Smile like you mean it!*

Jennifer/Jessica/Juniper and her blisters finally disembarked onto the sidewalk. For someone with such painful blisters, her hip-swaying gait hadn't suffered. Marco seemed to be making a similar observation.

As if reading her mind, Marco gave the front seat a pat. "Come on up." He grinned.

*Dammit. That grin.*

After buckling her seat belt, she turned to face him. In unison, they both said, "I'm sorry." They laughed. Then, as if that weren't bad enough, they both asked, "For what?" When he laughed, everything she'd been worried about disappeared.

Because they were such good friends!

Lydia said, "Me first. I was grouchy this morning. The water was off, which ruined my hair, and I always get nervous on the first day of class." *Gee, Lydia, spill your guts, why don't you? Did you leave anything out? I'm sure he'd love to hear about your periodontal pocket depth.* She exhaled in disgust.

He made a face as if she were talking crazy. "Grouchy? I didn't notice."

Lydia thought for a second. "How could you not notice? Do I come across like that all the time?"

He glanced at her with amusement in his eyes. "No, I was just being nice." That grin again. He could say pretty much anything, and if he followed up with that grin, she would be fine with it. "I just figured it was a female thing."

If she hadn't been dazzled by his smile, she might have taken offense instead of saying, "Oh, no. That was two weeks ago." *Mental facepalm!* "I'm sorry. I can't believe I just said that." *I mean, I really can't believe I just said that.*

Marco took it in stride. "That's okay. It kind of feels like having a sister."

Lydia forced a smile. *Great.*

# CHAPTER THREE

Eve brought two cups of coffee to her desk while Caroline waved goodbye to her clients. Once they were out of sight, Caroline said, "That went well. They're buying one of the two. They just need to decide which one. They told me to expect a call in the morning."

"That's fantastic!"

Caroline collapsed in her desk chair and rolled it over to Eve's desk. "I'm exhausted."

Eve handed her one of the coffees. "Take a break."

"I like the way you think." Caroline proceeded to update her on the day's events. "So that was my day. How was yours?"

Eve took a sip of her coffee then looked Caroline in the eye. "Not nearly as good as yours."

"Oh? What happened?"

Eve was finishing her account of the plumbing

visit when Marco's SUV pulled up in front. Lydia walked in, an unreadable look on her face. "Hi."

Eve had expected a bit more than that, so as Lydia walked past her, Eve said, "How was your day?"

"Fine." With that, her daughter disappeared to the back and headed upstairs.

Eve lifted her eyebrows. "Well, that was informative."

Caroline smiled gently. "She reminds me of what it was like to be young."

Eve reflected on life at eighteen. "At her age, I had a baby."

"And look what you've done."

"Yeah. Her first day of college. She's an adult. I should feel relieved. I mean, when I gave birth to her, I was overwhelmed by the responsibility. I'd lost my freedom—my life. But now, here I am. Mission accomplished. So I should feel happy, right?"

"Seeing Dylan couldn't have helped."

"It had to happen eventually. It's amazing it hasn't before now. I know he moved out of town, but he still works here with his dad." Her voice trailed off as she detected something in Caroline's expression. She had a pretty good poker face, but Eve knew her too well.

Caroline confessed. "Not so amazing."

Eve narrowed her eyes. "Why?"

Caroline stared at her coffee then looked up. "When the plumbing issues began, I don't know who brought it up first. Owen and I had a kind of mutual understanding that he wouldn't send his son here unless he couldn't help it. Apparently today, he couldn't help it."

Eve wasn't surprised. "Owen's retiring, so it's going to be Dylan from now on."

Caroline thought for a moment. "We could change plumbers."

"No, Dylan doesn't deserve that. It was such a long time ago. We've moved on, I think."

Caroline had a way of being sympathetic without making Eve feel uncomfortable. "Still, why don't I just ask around?"

"No. That would be awkward for you and unfair to him."

"But today upset you."

"I wouldn't say 'upset.' It was just a surprise."

Caroline set down her coffee. "Well, mull it over. We can touch base tomorrow." She looked at her watch. "You know what? I've just got a few loose ends here to tie up, but why don't you call it a day? Order some Chinese—my treat. I'll call and tell them to charge it to me. You go see how Lydia's doing."

Eve tried to protest. "Caroline..."

"No. It's not up for discussion."

Eve exhaled. "Thank you."

Caroline waved her hand toward the door. "Now, shoo! I've got work to do." She rolled her chair back to her desk and logged on to her computer.

Eve glanced at Lydia's closed bedroom door. *She'll come out later for food.*

She looked at the clock on the kitchen wall. *Four o'clock.* It was a little bit early for wine, but who was here to judge her? She poured herself a glass and went out to the deck. Just past the tree-tops was the harbor. How many times had she come out here and found solace in this view?

Nearly at their peak color, the leaves rustled as a cool autumn breeze blew in from the sea. Change was in the air. Lydia was beginning a new phase in her life, and now Dylan was back in Eve's life—if being her plumber counted as that. Seeing him felt oddly familiar, despite being an unsettling reminder of a time when life had stopped being simple.

She had been younger than Lydia when she went to a party and found herself chatting with Jack Watkins. They'd been in a number of classes together, but they hadn't spoken more than a few words to each other. That night, he'd been drinking, but he seemed okay. Eve had drunk a few wine coolers, but she couldn't blame it on that. Jack had just broken up with his girlfriend and was suddenly paying attention to Eve.

Athletic and confident, Jack was the kind of guy people noticed. Everyone liked him, and anyone with him tended to fade into the background. If Jack had a best friend, Dylan was it. Looking back, Eve recalled certain things more clearly—like Dylan. He'd been at that party. She'd barely noticed him then. All she'd noticed was Jack and how focused he was on her. The attention had gone to her head.

Eve had a curfew, but her ride home was nowhere to be found. Jack offered to drive her, so she took him up on his offer. When they got to the car, he told her he liked her. He kissed her. She hadn't expected it. Maybe that was what made her stop thinking clearly. Ordinarily, she was a practical sort. But the whole evening had been so unexpected. Until that night, she'd never been sure if Jack even knew who she was. So when he showed some interest, she liked how it felt. Being with him made the world fade away until only the two of them mattered.

While Jack started the car, someone slapped a hand against the driver's side window. They both turned to look. It was Dylan. He was yelling at Jack. With a laugh, Jack looked over at Eve. "Let's get out of here."

Then he backed out of the driveway and left Dylan behind. They drove into the hills and stopped on a quiet stretch of the country road, where he kissed her again. Jack made her body come to life, and she wanted more. By the time he dropped her off at home, Eve was in love. She and Jack were a couple for a week—until his ex-girlfriend decided she wanted him back.

He said, "Sorry, Eve." And with that, her first love was over.

Dylan's locker was a few down from hers, and he heard the whole thing. Eve watched Jack walk away. As she turned back to her locker, their eyes met. Dylan looked like he wanted to say something, but Eve opened her locker and hid her face in it. She managed to pull it together enough to go on to her next class.

It had never been love. If only she'd realized it at the time. Six weeks later, suddenly sick, she shut her locker and ran to the bathroom. When she came out, Dylan was waiting. The bell rang, and they were alone. He didn't pry. In fact, he didn't talk at all. He just walked her to class. A few days later, she felt sick during a class both Jack and Dylan were in, and she ran out of the room. Dylan caught up with her in the nurse's office. By then, it didn't take a genius to figure it out. He never asked, but she was sure he knew. Until then, they'd been more acquaintances than friends, but that day was a turning point in their friendship.

The months that followed were a blur of angry parents, homeschooling, and visits from Dylan. One day after school, when her parents were still at work, Dylan stopped by the house to see how she was doing.

She invited him in. A few minutes later, he asked her to marry him. It was simple, straightforward, and completely unromantic at a time when she wasn't feeling too kindly toward men. Who did he think he was, riding in on his white horse to rescue her? Had she asked to be rescued?

Her father arrived home to find them arguing, or rather Eve yelling at Dylan. Her father assumed Dylan must be the father, and everything went downhill from there. He punched Dylan. To his credit, Dylan didn't try to stop him. He simply took it and, with a sideways glance at Eve, left.

Eve's father dragged her to the car, and her mother joined them. They went to Dylan's house and all sat while the adults decided the rest of their lives. Except no one asked Eve. Dylan appeared surprisingly calm in light of the assumption they'd all formed. When it got to the point of choosing the wedding date, Eve stood and said, "No!"

They all turned and stared.

"This is my baby, and I'll decide when to marry." She was on the brink of telling them that Dylan wasn't the father. She should have. But that would have brought Jack back into her life. No, this was her life and her baby. No one, not Jack and not Dylan, could have either.

Dylan stepped toward her. "Eve? Could we talk?"

She glared at him. "Why? I don't understand what you're trying to do—"

"Help you."

"I don't want your help! I don't want any of this!" She stormed out of Dylan's house, which was all very bold and dramatic until she realized she had nowhere to go and no way to get there. But she started to walk.

A few minutes later, her parents pulled up alongside her. "Get in, Eve." And she did.

She didn't marry Dylan. When his parents offered to pay child support, she sent them a letter and told them the truth—at least the part about Dylan not being the father. They never spoke to her or her parents again. But when word spread through the small town that she'd had the baby, Dylan stopped by with a panda bear.

"I've gone to work for my father."

"That's good." She meant it. In the months since she'd seen him, she'd had time to think, and she finally saw he'd been trying to help her.

"Eve, I can afford to support us."

"Us?"

"And I'd be a good father to Lydia."

"Dylan..." She felt like she ought to say thank you, but all she could see at that moment was one more person trying to take control of her life.

Then he said, "I love you."

"No, you don't." Having a baby was a big enough change in her life. She couldn't marry a man she didn't love. Love? She barely knew him. "I know you're trying to help, but I've got to do this myself."

He didn't argue. They must have said more to each other, but all Eve remembered was that he left. He left, and she didn't see him again for years.

But that danged panda bear became Lydia's favorite possession.

# CHAPTER FOUR

Colored leaves glistened with dew on the trees lining Main Street as Caroline walked into the office and closed the door on the brisk autumn air. She went straight to Eve's desk and set down two cups of coffee and a small paper bag. "Pumpkin spice coffee and—"

Eve interrupted. "You didn't!" She peeked inside the bag. "Yes, it is! My favorite apple cider doughnuts. Oh! They're still warm." She inhaled their scent then lifted starry eyes to Caroline but was met with a serious look.

"Let's talk."

"Uh-oh. My favorite coffee and fresh doughnuts? That doesn't bode well."

"Don't worry. I just wanted to run something by you." Caroline sat down and scooted her chair next to Eve's desk.

Eve sipped her coffee and braced herself.

"I talked to Dylan. The plumbing needs to be replaced."

*Is that all?* "Sounds expensive."

"Yes, but it has to be done. What concerns me is how it will affect you."

"Well, I'm not going to lie. I'm a big fan of indoor plumbing."

Caroline laughed. "Me too. The thing is, it'll take about a week."

"Well, like you said, it has to be done."

"The question is, by whom?"

"By Dylan, apparently."

With a wince, Caroline lifted her shoulders.

"A week?"

"He'd be in your apartment, possibly cutting into your walls and floors."

"I've just put up my fall decorations." But that wasn't what really concerned Eve. She took a few moments to think. Seeing Dylan brought back so many feelings she'd tried to forget. But he hadn't done anything wrong. He was just part of a difficult memory.

Caroline assured her, "I could get someone else."

"No. That wouldn't make sense. He's local, and we trust him."

Caroline nodded.

Eve exhaled. "It's not like we'd be together that much. I'd be down here when he's working. Maybe it's better this way. It would force us to get used to each other and make things less awkward. Right?"

Caroline's eyebrows furrowed. "It could. But there's no pressure. It's your decision."

It was thoughtful of Caroline to give her a choice, but having to find someone new was a lot to ask, even if they were good friends. *And really, it's only a week. How bad could it be?* "I'll be fine. Let's do it."

Caroline smiled. "Okay, then. I'll give him a call."

DYLAN WAS at Eve's door at seven thirty the next morning. "I'm sorry. Lydia's still getting ready. She's not quite a morning person. Neither am I. Excuse me." While Dylan set down his toolbox, Eve went to the bathroom and tapped on the door. "Lydia, Dylan's here."

"Dylan who?"

Eve cast an embarrassed glance at Dylan then spoke through the closed door. "The plumber. Remember? I told you he was coming today."

"Just a minute!"

Dylan waited patiently. "Should I have come later?"

"No. Well, maybe. We're kind of locked into a schedule with her school and my work."

"If seven thirty is too early, how about eight?"

Eve smiled. "Yes. We could be out of your way by then." She started to pick up her coffee then said, "I'm sorry. Would you like a cup?"

Before he could answer, she poured one and gave it to him.

He thanked her then took a sip, and silence settled.

Eve glanced toward the bathroom. "I'll just check on Lydia." She arrived at the door just as Lydia opened it. Clutching her makeup bag, she said, "Sorry!" Then she rushed to her room and grabbed her bookbag. As she emerged and headed for the stairs, Eve stopped her. "Lydia, this is Dylan."

"Hi!" She thrust her hand to his and gave it a quick shake as a car horn sounded below. "That's Marco. Gotta go!"

The door slammed, and she was gone.

Dylan was still staring at the door when Eve said, "That was Lydia."

He looked at Eve with a warmth that caught her off guard. "She looks a lot like you did at that age."

Eve had thought that herself, but to hear it from Dylan as he gazed at her like that brought unexpected emotions to the surface. He seemed to be recalling the past as vividly as she was. She said, "That was a long time ago."

A wistful smile came and went quickly. "You did it, Eve."

She couldn't trust herself to voice the question, but he seemed to understand and went on to explain. "You told me you wanted to do it yourself, and you did it. She's a beautiful girl."

Long-pent-up emotions flooded her as she looked into his eyes. "Thank you." She lost herself in his gentle gaze for far too long then inhaled with forced cheer. "Well, the kitchen's here, where we're standing, and the bathroom's in there. So just make yourself at home." She looked away and frowned. *Make yourself at home?* "I'll be downstairs if you need anything." She tried not to look like she was fleeing, but that was exactly what she was doing. At the foot of the stairs, she stopped and touched her cheeks with the back of her hand. She felt flushed and completely out of control.

Caroline was busy at her desk when Eve sat down and shuffled some papers. She tried to work, but her mind was on Dylan.

"Everything okay?" Caroline asked without looking up.

"Yeah. Dylan's upstairs getting started."

"So it's going to work out okay?"

Eve nodded enthusiastically. "Oh yeah."

"Good."

*Yeah, everything's going to be fine. Just fine.*

Eve kept busy all morning—or tried to. But her mind kept wandering back to Dylan. It didn't help that he kept coming downstairs to get things from his truck. Then she would sit uneasily, trying to look unperturbed until he passed by the doorway on his way upstairs. Each footstep drew her attention from her work, until she felt practically useless. It was all she could do to give the appearance of work and conceal her distraction from Caroline.

Caroline shuffled some papers then stacked them and slipped them into her satchel. A couple walked into the shop. Caroline greeted them then left for an afternoon of house viewing.

As the door closed, Eve sighed. She leaned back and released all the tension she'd held in all morning. A light tap on the doorframe startled her and brought it all back.

Dylan stuck his head in the door. "I'm going to the deli for some lunch. Can I get you anything?"

*Lunch?* In all the disruption of her morning routine, she'd completely forgotten about lunch. She was still forming an answer when Dylan said, "I'll bring you a sandwich. What'll it be? Ham and cheese? BLT?"

"Tuna."

"Okay. Be right back." Seconds later, the outside door closed.

*Tuna?* She hadn't meant to say that. She'd been trying to think of a plausible excuse to avoid having lunch with him. But instead, she just answered his question. This was not working out like she'd expected it to.

While a fresh pot of coffee brewed, Eve paced. She'd expected a little tension, but this went beyond that to a sense of something unspoken between them. What it was or where it came from, she couldn't understand.

In those days long ago, they'd been on the periphery of each other's circles, spending time together but never being close enough to say more than small talk. She didn't remember the faraway look in his eyes, but it drew her in until she thought she might lose herself in the depth of his gaze. Back then, she would surely have noticed a look like that.

*Wouldn't I?* Flashes of memory of the night she'd been with Jack returned. Dylan was there. Just before she and Jack left together, Jack had leaned close to Dylan and said something. They'd exchanged harsh words. At the time, Eve had dismissed it. Their argument hadn't concerned her. Only Jack had mattered. He'd laughed it off, hooked his arm about Eve's neck, and led her away.

The coffee sputtered as it finished dripping. Eve filled her cup and sat down at her desk. *This was a bad idea.* Maybe she should just be honest with Dylan and tell him it wasn't working out. He was too much of a reminder of a time in her life that she would rather forget.

"Tuna sandwich." Dylan walked in and set Eve's sandwich on her desk. "Mind if I join you?"

*Yes.* "No. There's a table in the back." She got up and followed him.

As they unwrapped their sandwiches, Eve decided to wait until they'd finished eating. Then she would tell him. That way, there wouldn't be any awkward fumbling with his food and his water bottle. When he was packed up, she would make a clean break. All that remained was figuring out what she was going to say.

Dylan took a bite of his sandwich then looked at hers. "I hadn't figured you for a tuna girl."

Eve lifted her eyebrows. "Really? I'm not sure what a tuna girl is, but I've been a devout fan of the deli's tuna for years. In high school, I used to put potato chips inside for texture, but nowadays, I opt for the more elegant tuna with lettuce."

He made a face.

"What?"

He shook his head dismissively. "There's no accounting for taste."

Her jaw dropped. "Says the man with the liverwurst sandwich. You know what they say. People who live in glass houses..."

"Eat liverwurst sandwiches? Hmm. Good to know."

Eve couldn't help but smile. For a fleeting moment, she felt almost as carefree as when she was at the high school lunch table. But then, Dylan was never at her table. He was always at Jack's.

"You grew awfully quiet."

Eve pulled herself back from her thoughts of the past and smiled. "I just, uh..." *I can't do this.* She looked at him frankly. "Being with you reminds me of the past."

He looked as though he knew the answer. "And not in a good way?"

She was about to answer when the front door opened, and a gust of wind blew papers from her desk to the floor. "Excuse me." Ignoring the papers, she greeted a couple who'd been walking by and thought they would inquire about properties in the area. Eve made an appointment for them to see

Caroline. When they were gone, she scooped up the papers and anchored them on her desk with the computer keyboard.

She returned to the table. "You can just smell the fall in the air—crisp autumn leaves and a cool breeze from the sea." She hoped he would forget what she'd said before, so they could return to pretending that everything was fine.

Dylan folded his arms and leaned back. He looked deep in thought, but not about crisp autumn leaves and brisk sea breezes. "It's been a long time. We don't have to go back there."

Eve tried to be cheerful, but the best she could manage was a wistful "I can't seem to help it." It was his fault. She looked at him, and she was there. And yet, knowing that, she looked at him. There was so much to say, but neither would, so they searched each other's eyes as if they might find an answer.

A loud knock on the back door tore Eve away. "Allie?" She got up and answered the door. Allie started to come in, saw Dylan, and stopped. After saying hello, Allie lowered her voice. "Sorry. I didn't know you had company."

Eve was about to explain that it was nothing, just lunch—in other words, a lie—but Allie said, "I was in the neighborhood and just thought I'd pop in to say hello."

Eve smirked. *In the neighborhood?* Allie lived next door.

Allie grew increasingly cheery. "Well, I came to

say hi, and I have. So... bye. We'll catch up later." She leaned to one side, gave Dylan a wave, then positioned herself out of his sight. With urgent, wide-open eyes, Allie tilted her head toward Dylan.

Eve moved into the doorway to fully block Dylan's view. "Thanks for stopping by. Bye, Allie." She made a face that was meant to convey something along the lines of *"Stop thinking whatever you're thinking and go. Now."*

With twinkling eyes, Allie grinned and gave Eve a double thumbs-up, then she made a big show of tiptoeing away.

Dylan said, "I've always liked Allie."

"Yeah. She's something." *Thumbs-up? Subtle. Really subtle.*

"I remember her from day camp."

The memory dawned on her. "That's right. I forgot that you were a day camp counselor."

"Now look at us–adults. When did that happen?"

Eve lost her smile. "I feel like I went from kid to adult in an instant."

Dylan's face filled with regret. "I'm sorry. I didn't mean to—"

"You didn't. I'm the one who went there. Sorry to bring the room down." To fill in a lengthening pause, Eve said, "Have you kept up with your friends?" Instantly, she regretted her words.

With a thoughtful nod, he said, "Most of them." He eyed her for a moment. "Except Jack."

Here they were, back in this place where she didn't wish to be. Without meaning to, she had done it to herself. Now she wasn't sure how to get out of it.

Dylan said, "Jack and I had a falling out. Then he went off to college in Boston, and he's never come back—at least not that I know of."

"I'm sorry. I thought you two were pretty good friends."

"Yeah, but some things are bigger than friendship."

Eve had never told anyone who Lydia's father was, but she'd always felt as though it were an unspoken secret between her and Dylan. As though nothing were wrong, she nodded and got up. "I'd better get back to work."

Eve threw out her trash from lunch and headed for her desk.

"It was you. We fought over you."

Eve stopped. She took a moment before she dared to turn and look at him.

Dylan stood on the other side of the doorway, gazing softly, then he looked away. "I didn't like... how he treated you. But I just made things worse." He smiled bitterly to himself then lifted his eyes to her. "I'm sorry about what happened between us—you and me."

Eve was too uneasy to respond.

He said, "I offended you when I should have left you alone, and I've always regretted it. For years, I've wanted to tell you I'm sorry, but—"

"You didn't offend me. I was... It was a difficult time. I wasn't thinking too clearly." Eve struggled to find the right words. "I'm sorry. I've regretted it too. What I should have said was thank you."

"In my clumsy way, I was trying to help. Someone needed to do the right thing."

*And Jack wouldn't.* Dylan was too kind to say it out loud. Eve felt unexpected relief to be able to acknowledge the truth. "I'm sorry I cost you a friend."

Dylan looked at her as though she didn't get it at all. "I gave up a friend because I could no longer respect him. You have nothing to be sorry for."

Sudden apprehension seized Eve as she realized she had as much as confirmed Jack was the father. As kind as Dylan seemed in the moment, it concerned her. At any moment, with one word of the truth, he could destroy the life she'd built with Lydia. This gave him power over her, and she wanted to plead with him not to betray her confidence. Doing so could bring Jack into their lives, which was the last thing Eve wanted.

Dylan said, "You look worried."

She started to deny it.

With a knowing look, he said, "It's been almost nineteen years. Have I given you any reason not to trust me?"

Caroline walked through the front door with her clients. They exchanged hellos, then after her clients had gone, Dylan gave her a plumbing update. When he'd finished, he said, "Well, work's calling."

"Like 'Danny Boy'?"

When his eyebrows drew together, Caroline said, "Sorry."

Whistling the song, he climbed the stairs.

Eve tried to work, but thoughts spun around in her head. Even if Jack learned the truth, it wasn't as if he could take away custody. Lydia was too old for that. But there were other ways she could lose Lydia than in court. If Lydia found out Eve had held back the truth, it could put a rift between them that might never be mended.

Kim popped in the door, full of cheer. "Hi! I'm on my way back from lunch, so I thought I'd remind you."

Eve tried to snap out of her mood, but she must have failed, because Kim said, "You didn't forget, did you?" Her eyes opened wide with frustration. "Apple picking. Tomorrow morning."

Eve took in a breath and assumed a cheery demeanor. "How could I forget?"

Kim looked satisfied with her answer. "I touched base with Allie. Caroline?"

"I'll be there."

"Yay! Girls' day out! Apple cider, doughnuts, and nature! It doesn't get any better than that!"

## CHAPTER FIVE

Eve, Caroline, Allie, and Kim sat at a picnic table, drinking coffee, with a half-empty box of doughnuts in the middle of the table.

Kim reached for a second doughnut. "Lydia doesn't know what she's missing. This is way more fun than homework."

Eve nodded. "Oh, absolutely! I'm sure she'd agree, but I gave birth to an overachiever."

Caroline said, "There's nothing wrong with that."

Allie was quick to agree. "She's a hard worker."

Eve couldn't disagree, but she worried. "Maybe too hard. I wonder if she's followed my example a little too well."

Allie thought for a moment. "I wouldn't worry. She'll be fine."

Kim laughed. "Marco will loosen her up."

Eve frowned. "I'm not sure that's a good thing."

"I didn't mean loosey-goosey, just... you know...

kick up her heels—not too far up." Kim shut her eyes. "Never mind."

Allie chimed in to rescue the moment. "Marco's a good guy, really."

"But?" Eve looked from one to the other as her level of concern worsened.

Caroline looked around. "Wow! This place is getting absolutely crowded! We'd better get moving before they pick all the good apples."

Allie downed the rest of her coffee, and they all headed down the path to the orchard. A half hour later, their bags were nearly full. As they rounded the end of a row of apple trees, Caroline smiled and waved. "Dylan!"

Looking outdoorsy in jeans and a flannel shirt, Dylan grinned. "Caroline, long time no see."

With a laugh, Caroline said, "You can't get rid of me, can you? So, who's your friend?"

With him stood a girl who looked about ten years old. "This is Hailey, my daughter."

Caroline shook Hailey's hand. "Hello, Hailey. It's nice to meet you."

Eve was surprised—more so than she thought she should be. He hadn't mentioned a daughter. *Does this mean he's married?* She wondered why she'd assumed that he wasn't.

When all of the introductions were complete, there was a lull. Kim jumped in with a not-too-subtle "Is Hailey's mother here somewhere?"

Eve wanted to swat her, but her curiosity took over.

He said, "It's my weekend with Hailey."

*Ah, divorced.* Eve sensed she wasn't the only one drawing that conclusion.

Another lull settled, then Caroline said, "Well, have fun, you two."

Dylan smiled at Eve. "See you Monday." As an apparent afterthought, he gave Caroline a nod.

They all said their goodbyes and headed in opposite directions. When they were well out of earshot, Kim practically sang, "See you Monday—Eve."

Eve shrugged. "What?"

Kim said, "He looked right at you."

"Because he's my plumber."

Kim said to herself, "I could use a new plumber. My pipes are a little rusty."

"We're just friends."

Kim lifted her eyebrows. "First, he's your plumber, and now, he's your"—she made air quotes—"friend."

Eve stared blankly while Allie and Caroline looked on, amused.

"Okay. Maybe you're friends for now. Let's touch base in a week."

Eve furrowed her brows.

Kim would not be deterred. "Come on, Eve! Like you haven't noticed. He's hot!"

Eve felt flustered. "He's just Dylan. I know him from school."

"Does 'just Dylan' have a just brother?"

"No."

Kim pouted. "That's too bad. I had such plans for us." She grabbed Eve's arm. "Oh!"

Eve flinched. "What?"

Kim's expression brightened. "You should make him a pie."

*Pie?* Eve pondered the random suggestion.

Folding her arms, Kim leaned closer. "Come on. I saw the two of you."

Eve raised her eyebrows. "Did you see Allie and Caroline? Because they were here too."

Kim slowly nodded as her eyes sparkled with a scheme.

Eve looked at Allie and Caroline, hoping one of them might rescue her, but they seemed to be on Kim's side.

Kim repeated, "Make him a pie."

"I'll make you a pie," Eve said, "for your face!"

Kim laughed. "Very funny. But seriously, when will you teach me your pie magic?"

"There's no magic. It's called a recipe."

Allie hooked her arm in Eve's. "So, ladies. Let's plan our attack on the food tents. How about Eve and I tackle the cider line—and I mean literally. I'm so thirsty, I'll mow them all down. You two line up for the burgers."

Caroline grinned. "Sounds like a plan."

Kim power walked into the lead. "Keep up, ladies! There's food on the horizon!"

Monday morning, Dylan arrived with his daughter in tow just as Lydia was heading out to meet Marco.

"I hope you don't mind," Dylan said. "Her mother had to work an extra shift, so I've got a helper today."

Lydia said, "She can hang out in my room."

Eve smiled at Dylan as Hailey went to Lydia's room, but it faded when Hailey exclaimed, "That's such a cute panda!"

"He's special," Lydia said. "He's been my best friend for as long as I can remember."

Eve couldn't help herself. Her eyes drifted to Dylan's. He looked down to conceal the soft look in his eyes.

Lydia pulled some books from the closet for Hailey, then a horn honked out front. "Marco's here. Gotta go." With a quick goodbye, Lydia hurried down the stairs.

Eve turned to Hailey. "There's some juice in the fridge. And I think I've got some cookies in the second drawer over there if you get hungry. See you later."

Dylan thanked her, and she headed down to the office.

Throughout the morning, Eve's mind wandered to the moment when Hailey had found Lydia's panda. If she'd had any doubt as to whether Dylan remembered, it was gone when she saw the look on his face. It had happened too quickly for Eve to react and conceal her emotions. Flooded with the memory of Dylan's proposal, she could do nothing but relive that moment in all of its turmoil.

It must have hurt him to be rejected so soundly. He had made an enormous, life-changing offer that had taken a great deal of compassion and selflessness. She should have at least understood that and been kinder, but she'd been blinded by panic. Raising a child was daunting, but adding marriage to someone she didn't love had tipped the scale. Looking back, she was sure she had done the right thing, but she would always regret hurting Dylan.

When lunchtime came, Caroline suggested they invite Dylan and Hailey to join them. Eve had no choice. If she said no, she would have to explain why. So she agreed, and they all ate together. To Eve's surprise, she and Hailey got along famously, bonding over their shared love of books. In the course of discussing Lydia's books, as well as some Eve had read at Hailey's age, they discovered a shared love of Gilbert Blythe.

Hailey said, "If only there were boys like that in real life. The boys in my grade are so boring."

Eve sympathized. "I think Anne felt the same way about Gilbert until they got older."

"I guess so." She thought for a moment. "But I can't imagine liking any boy at my school like that." She wrinkled her face.

"Maybe not. But sometimes things change. People change." As Eve looked at Hailey, she felt a bit wistful for the days she and Lydia had talked of such things.

Hailey said, "Did you and Daddy know each other in school?"

That caught Eve off guard.

"We did," Dylan said with a smile.

Hailey grinned. "So, was he like your Gilbert Blythe?"

Eve felt a blush coming on. "No. Not exactly." She quickly added, "We just knew of each other."

"And had friends in common," Dylan said. He looked at Eve.

*Why would he do that—bring up Jack?* Eve got up and went to the counter to make coffee—not that she wanted any, but it gave her an excuse to escape.

Caroline asked, "How's the plumbing?"

Eve exhaled, grateful for the subject to move to safer ground. While Dylan explained the details, Eve's takeaway was that the water would be off for a couple of days, which gave her a couple of days away from Dylan to clear her head. Just when she'd begin to feel comfortable with him, something unexpected would hurl them back to the past.

When she'd regained her composure, Eve returned to the lunch table. By then, everyone had finished eating.

Caroline stood. "So, we'll move out this afternoon. I'll shift some appointments around, and Eve and I will work from my home."

Eve's mood brightened. "Sounds like a plan."

As they headed back into the office, Caroline said, "Don't forget your coffee."

"Oh, right." Eve went back to retrieve it.

WITH EVE GONE, Dylan was better able to concentrate on his work. When he took the job, he'd expected some tension between them but thought it would ease up in time. After all these years, they should've been able to move on and perhaps even be friends. But it felt as though they had been trapped in emotional limbo. Eve had done what she set out to do, and she'd done it well. She had every reason to feel content with her life, but when Dylan was with her, the tension between them was almost as strong as it ever had been.

Dylan doubted himself. Was it all on his side? After all, what did Eve have to feel awkward about? She had merely received an unwanted proposal, while Dylan had fallen in love. He should never have let it happen. He knew she was out of his league. Jack used to tease him about his inevitable career as a plumber—a chick magnet, he would call Dylan as he had a good laugh. The fresh smell of sewage drove all the girls mad. Dylan had laughed —on the outside. But he couldn't stay mad. It was Jack—his best friend. It was all in good fun.

Once, in a weak moment, he'd confessed to liking Eve. That had been a mistake. Jack was so innately competitive, he couldn't help himself. So, soon after, when his girlfriend broke up with him, Jack had cornered Eve at a party.

When Eve became pregnant, Dylan confronted Jack, but he'd denied it. They'd fought. He'd thought if Jack wouldn't do the right thing, he would—and he had. But Eve wouldn't have him. Soundly rejected, he'd convinced himself that it couldn't have been love after all. He had merely developed a crush—a significant crush—but a crush, nonetheless, which would fade in time. But it never did.

He'd moved on and gotten married, but that hadn't helped. Early on, they'd both known something was missing, but they'd tried to make it work. They'd had Hailey. Dylan loved her more than life, but it didn't change anything with her mother. It was Hailey's mother who'd finally ended the marriage. Dylan had no regrets. He loved Hailey too much for that. But in the five years that had followed, he'd settled back into the life he knew best—life alone.

## CHAPTER SIX

THE FOLLOWING WEDNESDAY, their lunch group met as it usually did, in the back room of Allie's shop. Eve and Caroline were working from Caroline's house while Dylan worked on the plumbing, but they drove over and picked up Kim on the way. They missed Lydia, but she was busy most days at school, so Allie closed the shop for the lunch hour.

As they walked in from the car, a sea breeze tossed colored leaves at their feet. Kim handed Allie the bag of sandwiches. "I've been dying to see what goes on at these secret lunch meetings."

Caroline put a finger to her lips. "Oh, it's all very hush-hush."

Allie lifted an eyebrow. "Very cloak-and-dagger."

Caroline nodded. "Or skull and bones."

"Yes." Eve helped Allie clear off the table. "We thought about making it formal—a secret society to take over government intelligence."

Caroline let out a laugh. "But we couldn't find any!"

Kim winced and groaned. "What's that smell?"

Eve narrowed her eyes as she opened a box. "That depends. Is it good?"

"Oh my gosh, it's amazing—like autumn and comfort."

"And maybe apples?" Eve pulled out a pie.

"That's it!" Kim bent down and slowly breathed in the scent of the pie.

Eve set the pie on the counter and sat down at the table. "I made a pie with the apples we picked."

Kim widened her eyes and pleaded pathetically, "For dessert? Please say yes."

Eve's eyes sparkled. "Oh, absolutely. It's your initiation into the lunch club. If you survive my cooking, you're in."

Kim said softly, "I am so lucky."

Eve unwrapped her sandwich. "Well, we'll see about that."

Halfway through lunch, the topic of plumbing came up, and that led to the topic of plumbers—Dylan, in particular.

Kim narrowed her eyes and spoke in a serious hush. "So, ladies, first off, what's the scoop? Is the plumber's crack really a thing?"

Eve's jaw dropped, while Caroline calmly smiled and nodded toward Eve. "I'll defer to my friend here, who's had more contact with him."

Eyebrows drawn together in a panic, Eve lifted flexed hands. "There hasn't been any contact!"

Kim looked triumphant. "But you looked!"

Eve's jaw was locked open. "I did not!" *Except for that one time.*

Kim gave Allie a wry look then looked back at Eve. "I'm not gonna lie. I did—at the apple orchard." She hastened to add, "At his butt. The plumber's crack remains unconfirmed. But the rest? If they gave out awards... Oh, do you think they do? I'd be a presenter!"

Eve watched and waited. There was no stopping Kim now.

Kim went on. "At conventions."

Eve wrinkled her face. "Kim."

Kim's eyes lit with enthusiasm. "The statues could be like the Oscars, only with jeans and a crack."

"No." Eve searched for an excuse. If she didn't stop Kim now, nothing good would come of this train of thought. She couldn't disagree with Kim's assessment, but... *No more buts!* Eve stood up. "Who wants pie?"

When they'd gone past the lunch hour by five minutes, they all stood hastily and cleaned up the lunch table.

Caroline looked at Allie and waved her away. "We've got this. Go open the shop."

"It's the off-season. Two minutes won't hurt."

Kim picked up the pie and stared at it as if it

were a rare and wondrous gem, if gems were large, pie-shaped, and surrounded by crust. "Farewell, the great love of my life." She took in a sharp breath. "Which reminds me!" She spoke with such a fervor that everyone stopped. Suddenly aware they were all staring, she said, "Dylan."

Eve squinted. "Are we suddenly calling out random names that we know?"

Kim looked at her frankly. With a quick turn, she went to the window. "His truck's there."

"That's nice." Eve was beginning to wonder about Kim.

Then Kim thrust the pie pan at Eve. "Take it to him."

Eve couldn't even manage a "huh?"

"Allie! Where's the foil? Never mind, here it is. No, it's too sticky and crinkly. Allie, have you got any new foil?"

Already on her way to the stairs, Allie said, "I'm on it."

She returned a minute later, and the two of them wrapped foil over the pan. Allie said, "Wait, I've got some paper plates somewhere."

"No!"

"No?" Now it was Allie's turn to look confused.

Kim explained patiently as if to a child. "If she gives him the pie tin—"

"She?" Eve asked.

"Then he'll have to return it."

Eve was adamant now. "No, he won't, because I'm not giving it to him."

Deep disappointment was etched in her friends' faces. In unison, they asked, "Why not?"

"Because..." *Good, Eve. Very convincing.*

"But you like him, don't you?" Caroline asked.

Eve couldn't answer. She didn't want to lie, but she didn't want to say the truth out loud. So she just looked back at them.

Something caught Kim's eye, and she rushed to the window. "He's loading his truck."

A sense of urgency rose from Eve's gut. *No, I couldn't.*

Allie looked sympathetic. "Kim, don't push her. If she doesn't feel that way for him..."

"But she does."

*Et tu, Caroline?*

Caroline quietly said, "Go give him some pie. It's not a bold declaration of love. It's a nice thing to do. So do it." She added a little hand gesture, as if Eve wouldn't understand otherwise.

Panic spread from Eve's heart to her brain. "I haven't really dated very much." *At all. I'm not ready for this.*

"It's a pie, not a date." By this point, Kim had parked herself at the window and was giving a play-by-play of Dylan's actions outside. "He's gone into the building again." She guided Eve by the shoulders to the door. "Wait right here. When I say to, go out and give this to him." She snapped her fingers. "Pie! Where's the pie?"

Allie rushed it to Kim, who in turn gave it to Eve.

"Okay, good. No, wait... Breathe... Think of a calm, tropical beach—Oh! There he is! Go!"

Eve froze. *I never really signed on for this.* Kim's insistence was hard to combat. Eve hadn't raised a child alone without developing a semblance of control over her life—something Kim had just destroyed in a matter of minutes. She didn't know how to cope.

"Go! He just reached for his keys!"

Evidently, Eve didn't have to know anything, because Kim reached over, opened the door, and gave Eve a shove between the shoulder blades. She was in flight—or at least on her way.

Dylan saw her and smiled.

*It's too late. He saw me. But he's smiling, so that's a good sign. And he's waiting.* She drew in a deep breath. *It's only pie. You are just being nice.*

With astonishing presence of mind, she stopped before running into him.

"Hi," he said. "I didn't expect to see you. I was just on my way out to lunch."

His searching expression made her nervous. "Here." She thrust it at him, jabbing his abs with the edge of the pie pan. Reflexively, he took hold of the pie—and her hands.

Managing to make eye contact, she said, "Sorry," and slipped her hands away. If only she'd gone out more over the years, just for practice. But those dates were different. She'd never felt like this.

He dismissed her apology with a slight shake of his head then looked down at the pie.

She said, "It's pie."

He looked pleased.

"I made it with apples." She frowned. *What?* "From the orchard the other day. I mean, I made it last night, but the apples..."

A spark lit his eyes as he nodded.

"We had two pieces left over from lunch."

He smiled as though something in all that made sense. "Thank you."

"You're welcome." She glanced back toward the office. "Well, I've got to get back."

He nodded. "Thanks again for the pie."

"Sure, no problem." She wanted to run, but she walked away. The door closed behind her, and the Vaughan Plumbing truck pulled out of the driveway.

Eve walked inside, where three pairs of eyes waited. She looked from one pair to the next. "What?"

Kim looked like a proud parent at a kindergarten recital. "So, you gave him the pie?"

Pleased but trying not to show it, she said, "I did."

Caroline tried to be the calm, reasonable one, but Kim's matchmaking seemed to have rubbed off on her. "He's a really nice guy—and he's really attractive!"

*Yup. Caroline has been replaced by a pod person.* Eve got her purse and pulled out her car keys. *Oh wait, I'm not driving.* She put them back in her purse. "So, I guess we should go?" She looked at Caroline, who was, in fact, driving.

Kim took a practical tone as she folded her arms and sat on the edge of the table. "I like him."

Eve lifted her eyes. "He's a likable guy."

Kim said, "I like him for you." With that, she stood, headed for the door, then paused with her hand on the doorknob. "Just make sure he washes his hands after work. Twenty seconds. Make it forty. I'll be in the car." She left before seeing Eve's horrified look.

As they pulled out of Allie's driveway, Caroline said, "Dylan's a great guy."

Eve nodded.

"And really good-looking," Kim added.

With a nod, Caroline said, "And nice."

"Yes, he is. All those things." Eve gazed out the window and said tersely, "Great guy, good-looking, and nice."

Caroline frowned. "Yeah. How dare I trash talk him like that?"

Eve exhaled. "Sorry."

Caroline smiled gently. "He likes you."

Eve tried not to frown, but she felt so uneasy. "I think I like him."

Kim cheerily joined in from the backseat. "He likes you. You like him. Yeah, I can see how that's a problem."

The source of Eve's worry, at least in part, was suddenly clear. "We've got too much baggage—and it's all the same brand."

Kim said, "Matching luggage is good."

Ignoring her, Eve said, "Too much has happened. I don't think we could ever get past it."

Caroline lifted her eyebrows. "Apple pie's a good start."

Eve felt the blood drain from her face. "I can't believe that just happened."

"I can." Kim smiled triumphantly.

Eve felt like she'd just lost her mind. "It's just too much. I'm not ready."

Kim pulled out her lip gloss and applied it while talking. "Putting things in perspective, all you did was give him some leftover pie. What's to get ready? Forks and napkins, maybe."

Caroline smiled at Kim in the rearview mirror. "Kim has a point. It's not a lifelong commitment. Yet."

Eve's phone chimed. "That must be Lydia." She pulled out her phone and felt the color drain from her face. "Dylan."

Caroline whipped her head toward Eve, who said, "Eyes on the road." Kim leaned forward as far as her seat belt would let her and looked over Eve's shoulder.

Eve felt like the sun had just come out and shone on her personally. She stared at the screen for a moment then looked at her friends. "He said, 'This pie is amazing.'"

"Translation—you're amazing." Kim leaned back and folded her arms. "Okay, full disclosure: that pie *is* amazing."

Caroline said, "Nobody texts that quickly just for pie."

Kim said, "Good point. That was quick. That's a guy for you. Either he just picked up a slice like it's pizza, or he's got a pie server in his truck."

Eve laughed. "He does have a lot of tools."

Kim's eyes twinkled. "Oh, I'm sure he does."

# CHAPTER SEVEN

SATURDAY MORNING, Eve was pouring her first cup of coffee when she received a group text message from Kim: *Emergency girls' night tonight. Silva Brothers' Brewpub. 8 p.m. sharp.*

Eve squinted and reread the message. *Emergency girls' night?* That was new. She went person-by-person, wondering whose emergency it might be. If it had been a family emergency, it wouldn't have kept until they could meet at a bar. So it had to be something of an emotional nature, which usually meant men. Caroline was between boyfriends and content, if not happy, about it. Allie and Theo Silva were a definite thing. If something had gone wrong with their relationship, they wouldn't be meeting at Theo's bar. Kim's social life was a challenge to keep up with. Her relationships were too light and breezy to rise to an emergency level. Eve was stumped. But something was wrong, and she would be there for her friends, because that was what they did for each other.

By the time evening came and Eve walked up to the Silva Brothers' entrance, she was bursting with curiosity. She pushed open the door and walked into the bar.

"Congratulations!" Not only was it the core group, but her daughter was also there, along with Theo, Marco, and Dylan. Theo and Marco owned the place, which gave them a good reason to be there. But Dylan? The only thing she could figure out was that he had happened to be there at the bar and had been drawn in, most likely by Kim.

Lydia bounced over to her mother and gave her a hug. Eve said softly, "Studying at the library?"

Lydia grinned. "Surprise! Congratulations!" Lydia pulled out a chair for her mother.

Caroline stood and lifted a glass of champagne in a toast. "For anyone who doesn't know, although I think I personally told each of you, Evelyn Parker has just passed her real estate exam." They applauded. Kim added a whistle, then Caroline continued. "Eve, in light of this professional triumph, I present this unofficial document fresh from my printer. Sorry, the official one hasn't arrived yet." She handed a homemade certificate to Eve, and more applause followed. "As of this moment, I am thrilled to offer my services as your mentor if you'll do me the pleasure of accepting a promotion from administrative assistant to real estate agent."

Eve was too stunned to speak.

"No pressure," Caroline said, "but I was kind of hoping that you would accept."

Eve quickly said, "Yes! Of course! I'm just... Thank you!"

The day before, Eve had shared the news with Caroline and been duly congratulated, but she'd never expected anything like this. Calls for a speech began, so Eve swallowed her natural shyness and did her best. "My career path hasn't exactly been typical, but I've wanted to do this for years. Yesterday, when I found out I'd passed, I was pretty ecstatic, so I went home and celebrated with a wine cooler on ice and some pizza. This is so much better. From now on, I'm putting Caroline in charge of my celebrations. Thank you, Caroline. And thanks, everyone, for sharing this with me."

Theo kept Eve's glass full while Marco played DJ. Lydia and Kim moved a couple of tables to make a makeshift dance floor, then they dragged Caroline along. They danced the first dance, then, before Eve was aware of what they were scheming, they dragged Dylan over to the dance floor.

*I should kill them right now. All of them.* But then her thoughts shifted to Dylan. He looked really good. She was so used to seeing him in his work clothes that she was surprised to see how well he cleaned up. The music cross-faded to a romantic ballad. *This is going to be awkward.* But then Dylan put his hand on the small of her back and took her other hand in his. She caught a faint whiff of cologne or perhaps shower gel.

Dylan said, "I'm not much of a dancer, but I think this is how it's done. Just in case, watch your feet."

She glanced up and found him smiling, then a movement in the periphery drew her attention. "They're staring at us."

"That's okay."

He looked so calm that Eve almost relaxed. "So you were in on all this?"

He smiled. "I was invited. I'm not crashing your party."

Eve couldn't help but laugh. "I know that. I meant it's a pleasant surprise—all of this is."

"You've got good friends."

"I do." Although she couldn't have agreed more, she still hadn't entirely ruled out killing them —in the nicest possible way. They were trying to fix her up with Dylan, and yet Dylan didn't seem to mind. Maybe she shouldn't mind, either. She certainly didn't mind how it felt to be close to him like this.

The song ended, and they parted. The last thing to slip away was his hand, and she missed it. The tempo picked up, and everyone swarmed the floor, except Eve. She felt flushed.

"Would you like to go out for some air?"

*How did he know? Oh no. Is my face beet red?* They went out to the rail overlooking the water but not before Kim caught her eye and lifted an eyebrow. Eve checked to be sure Dylan had missed it.

Once outside, they leaned on the rail and took in the view of the harbor. "I thought you could use a minute outside, where it's quiet."

"Yeah, I could, actually."

"I remember how you used to step out during parties. You're not a big people person, are you?"

"No. I'm surprised that you noticed."

"Not in a creepy way. But we went to a lot of the same parties. You get used to how people are, you know?"

"No, I don't know what you're talking about, Mr. Peels Pepperoni off of Pizza."

He threw his head back and laughed. "I hate the stuff. But I thought I was being discreet."

She smiled. "You were, sort of. I just didn't understand it. It's like scraping the icing off cake and then just eating the cake."

"I'm sure there must be people who do that."

With a half a nod, Eve said, "I'm sure you're right. I don't understand them either."

He chuckled, then it grew quiet. Oddly, Eve didn't mind it. In fact, as she listened to the water lap against the breakwater, she felt completely at peace. It was one of those perfect moments in life where everything was as it should be.

The water reflected the moon like a shimmering ribbon. "The moon's nearly full." When Dylan didn't respond, she turned to find his eyes on her.

He didn't even pretend to look at the moon. "Eve, I'm glad it's worked out so well for you."

"Thanks."

He lowered his gaze and smiled to himself.

It was the kind of autumn night when a cool breeze gently blew off the water, prompting couples to cling together for warmth—the kind of night when people kissed. As she gazed at Dylan, it seemed as though he felt it too. Eve averted her eyes and looked back at the water. She couldn't do it. Kissing Dylan went against every bit of good sense she had left on this perfect fall evening.

Dylan looked back toward the door. "This night air will go to your head if you let it. I think we've had enough. Shall we?"

He gestured toward the door, and they both went inside.

Theo slipped away from the party to tend to the bar. Allie followed and sat on a stool, gazing back at the party. "I'd say the party is a success."

Theo smiled as he poured two drafts. "So is Eve. She looks happy."

"Yeah, I think she is. But I wish she had more to her life than Lydia and work." She waited while Theo delivered the beers to some bar patrons. He returned, and she continued her thought. "With Lydia grown and in college, that just leaves work, and that isn't enough."

"What's the deal with Dylan?"

"I'm not sure. Caroline invited him. He did some work on her building last week. He and Eve go way back. That's all I know—except there's a spark there, and I think they'd be great together. I'd hate to see her miss out on a chance to be happy. Lydia's grown now. It's Eve's turn."

Dylan leaned his elbows on the bar. "In my experience as a bartender-slash-therapist, things have a way of working out the way they're supposed to."

Allie tilted her head, unconvinced. "Sometimes things need a little help."

Theo's mouth curved up at the corners. "You didn't seem to need any help walking into the men's room that time. And look how we've turned out."

Allie looked up as if asking for patience. "That was different. That was fate—and my unfortunate inattention to detail."

"Well, lucky for Eve, she's got three good friends with a take-no-prisoners approach. Poor Dylan will either end up with her on his own, or they'll hog-tie him to an altar somewhere."

Allie's jaw dropped. "That's so unfair! Although I wouldn't put it past Kim to try hog-tying him. But I'd never allow it. I'm too classy."

Allie waited for Theo to stop laughing. "I think that Caroline's clever enough to convince him that it was his idea."

Theo glanced at Caroline. "I can't disagree."

Marco emerged from the kitchen. "The kitchen's officially closed." Theo went to take care of some patrons while Marco washed glasses. "So, how's the party going?"

Allie glanced over at her friends, who were laughing as much as they were dancing. "Why don't you go see for yourself?"

Marco shook his head, but Allie persisted. "There's a distinct shortage of male dance partners over there."

Marco looked surprised. "You want to dance?"

Allie let out an exasperated sigh. "Not me, goofus. Let's see..." She looked across the room at her friends. Dylan and Eve were sitting close but not talking. Caroline and Kim were laughing, and Lydia had taken over as DJ. She was clearly the only one alone. Allie looked knowingly at Marco. "Ask Lydia."

"No. That's not a good idea."

Seeing he was serious, Allie asked, "Why?"

"I like Lydia. But I don't want to lose her as a friend."

"Are you that bad of a dancer?" She smiled, but he didn't seem to share her amusement.

He looked down and shook his head. "I'm that good of a friend. I wouldn't be good for her... in that way."

"Dancing?" Allie was beginning to wish she hadn't suggested it, although now she was curious.

Marco looked straight at her. "Sometimes I just get a vibe."

"From Lydia?"

Marco rolled his eyes. "Yes, from Lydia!"

"Oh." Allie leaned back and considered. *How have I been so clueless?* She worked with the girl, and she had no idea. Lydia had convinced her that they were just friends, like she once was with Justin. *Oh. So Lydia has feelings for Marco—or at least Marco thinks she does. And he doesn't return them.*

He said, "I wouldn't hurt her for anything."

"I know you wouldn't." While Marco loved the ladies, he wasn't the sort to lead someone on in a way that would hurt her. And Lydia was the sort who could be hurt.

"Well, the least you could do is give the poor girl a break. She's been trapped over there playing music for an hour."

"You're right." Marco took off his apron and walked over to her. He said something, and she smiled then headed toward Eve's table.

On her way over, a young guy who looked about Lydia's age approached her and asked her to dance. She took a moment to answer then nodded. *Good for her.* Allie hadn't expected Lydia to agree, nor had she expected Marco to watch so intently.

"Hey, you." Theo left the bartending to Melanie and came out from behind the bar. He took Allie's hand and led her to the dance floor. "Excuse me while I go bribe the DJ to play something slow and romantic."

Closing time came, and they finished cleaning and packing up to go, except for Lydia, who was helping Marco pack up the audio equipment. As she carried a speaker past her mother, Lydia said, "You go ahead. I'll be out in a minute."

Dylan said, "I'll walk you out to your car."

Eve thanked him, gave her friends a hug, and left. As they walked together, she tried to convince herself he was just being gentlemanly, but electricity arced between them. She hadn't felt like this before—ever. It was probably the excitement of the evening and her promotion. It couldn't be romance.

For eighteen years, Eve had punished herself for one night's indiscretion. From that point, she'd vowed to make all the right choices, and she had succeeded. Her career was on track. Lydia was amazing. But along the way, while convincing herself that it wasn't for her, Eve had entirely turned from romance. Now here she was with a man. Poised at the intersection of safety and love, she didn't want to go either way.

Whatever wall they had torn down between them was back. As though at any minute, they might lose their footing, they proceeded with care.

Eve stopped by her car door. "Here we are."

The moon and a distant building's floodlight lit their features enough for her to see Dylan was smiling. "Congratulations again."

"Thank you." She was happy about reaching

her career goal, but when she looked at Dylan, something more overshadowed her sense of accomplishment. The static electrical charge that she felt in his presence set off every inner alarm she possessed. It was the same heady feeling she'd experienced with Jack. Overpowering emotions like that had made her lose control once, and that once was enough to convince her how dangerous it was. Nothing good came from losing control.

Despite her better sense, she couldn't bring herself to look away. So she gazed at Dylan as though time and good sense didn't matter. Once more, Eve felt as though he might kiss her. When he didn't, she convinced herself she was imagining all of it. Maybe he'd been thinking of asking a question—searching for something to fill in the silence. That thought disappointed her. She had no business longing for his kiss. She had a good life. One kiss was not worth risking everything she'd worked for. But that wasn't it. She was risking her heart.

*I'm overthinking it all. This is simply a case of the jitters.* She'd deliberately avoided relationships over the years, and this was the logical outcome. She was unable to talk to a man. In her early twenties, she went on a couple of dates. They were fix-ups with no real chemistry. But Dylan made her heart come to life. He didn't even have to touch her for that sense of connection to make the air hum.

As they stood by her car, he glanced at her hair, then his eyes swept down her face as he put a hand on her shoulder. His touch made her practically dizzy. She couldn't help herself. She lifted her chin. His lips parted. Hers too.

The front door of the brewpub flung open, and laughter and people spilled out to the parking lot. Whatever might have happened between them was not going to happen. He slipped his hand from her shoulder as they both turned toward the commotion, and the moment was gone.

As Lydia joined them, Dylan said goodbye to them both and went to his truck. With a sigh, Eve sank into her car seat. The moment was gone. She was back in control. Well, not quite, but almost. Still, she wished he had kissed her.

# CHAPTER EIGHT

Dylan pulled onto the road and headed for home, wishing he could kick himself, but he couldn't do that while he was driving. *When are you going to learn?* A broken heart and a failed marriage later, here he was. As if all roads led to Eve, he couldn't help himself. He had loved her back then, and he still loved her now. *What kind of a fool lets that happen?*

But how could he help it? The dance and the moonlight, the warmth of her gaze—he was only human. If she weren't so amazing, he might stand a chance. But maybe, just maybe, he did already. Was it delusional to think they could be happy together? She'd seemed happy when they were dancing. Her laughter alone made life brighter. He could live on her laughter—with her in his arms.

After spending the drive home recalling each moment he'd spent with Eve, a thought came to mind. He was glad Caroline had included him in

Eve's celebration, but why had she invited him? It was small—close friends only—and he hadn't seen her in years. And then it was only because she'd needed a plumber. She hadn't expected him to answer the call. For years, his father had managed all of Eve's and Caroline's calls. The fact that Dylan had happened to answer the call wasn't remotely enough to warrant an invitation to Eve's party. And yet he'd received one. At the time, he hadn't thought much about it and had assumed she'd asked anyone she saw who knew Eve. It was only after the party was in full swing that he realized he was the only outsider. He was glad to be there, if for no other reason, to see Eve so happy. But he couldn't help but wonder what had prompted Caroline to invite him. Could this mean Eve had feelings for him? It gave him reason to hope.

EVE WAS glad she had work to focus on. Otherwise, the week would have been excruciatingly long. Even with her work routine disrupted by the temporary change of location, her thoughts managed to wander to Dylan. *What if we could be together? Thirty-five isn't that old. It could happen. But then why are we so out of sync? Love shouldn't be so hard. Whoa, wait a minute. Who said anything about love?*

She'd liked it the first couple of days Dylan was

working in her apartment while they were both there. It wasn't as though they'd even talked very much. Just hearing him walking around overhead had warmed her heart. Every clang of a wrench on a pipe had made her glad he was there. *Which is so sad for you, Eve. This is exactly what teenagers do—which you're not. You're a grown-up. You're a strong and independent woman. You don't need a man! But I want one.* Eve shuddered. *Snap out of it!* She leaned toward the monitor and buried her thoughts in her work.

By Friday afternoon, they were ready to call it a day when Caroline turned off her computer and swiveled her chair to face Eve. "Why don't you just ask him out?"

"What? Where did that come from?"

Caroline smiled gently. "From watching you two at your party last week and from the look on your face when you sit at your desk and stare out the window."

Eve said, "Maybe I just like the view."

Caroline looked over her glasses.

Eve's shoulders slumped. "I'm sorry."

"Sorry? You work harder than I do—almost. That's a high bar." She grinned. "You're misunderstanding. This isn't your boss complaining. This is your friend saying he likes you."

Eve felt a frown forming. She hadn't realized she'd been so transparent. *Does he?*

"And you like him."

Eve wanted to deny it, but she couldn't, so she gave up and let her guilt show on her face.

Caroline continued, "So... ask him out. Women can do that. It's the twenty-first century."

The mere thought of asking him out made Eve want to reach for a paper bag to breathe into. She could only shake her head slowly.

"You two look good together."

"Which makes us perfect for catalog ads, but..."

The doorbell rang, and Caroline got up to answer it. "I've got to stop shopping online. It's like Santa pulls up every day with a gift. Wait till you see the new shoes I've ordered." She opened the door. "Dylan!"

Eve took a few quick calming breaths. She wished she'd put on some lipstick before he'd arrived. Why hadn't she gone on more practice dates over the years, so she would be cool and collected like all of her friends? Instead, a man walked through the door, and she was a socially awkward thirtysomething disaster with moist palms and dry lips.

"Come on in." Caroline led him into the dining room, where they'd set up shop for the week.

Dylan smiled at Eve. "Hi."

"Hi. How are you?"

"Fine."

Caroline interrupted. "Oh, you know, I just remembered I've got a conference call in two minutes. Did you need something, Dylan?"

"No, actually, I came to see Eve." He held up the pie tin.

"Oh, that's nice." She glanced at her watch. "Sorry. Gotta go." She turned to Eve, phone in hand. "I'll just take this upstairs." She called over her shoulder, "Good to see you, Dylan."

*Conference call?* Eve tried to catch Caroline's eye, but she rounded the corner and disappeared up the stairs.

Looking almost as stunned as Eve, Dylan took a moment then held out the pie tin. "I'm returning this. Thanks for the pie. It was amazing." He grinned.

"You're welcome." She reached for the pie plate just as he moved it toward her. They couldn't touch. If her fingers even brushed against his, she would lose... something. *Control? Consciousness? Undergarments?* She couldn't trust herself. A week of daydreaming about him had made it all worse. She wasn't sure, but in the week since she'd seen him, she seemed to have worked up a full-blown crush on the guy with no further input from him.

She did her best impression of a woman whose breath hadn't been taken away. "Well, thanks for returning this." *Okay, Eve, we have thoroughly covered the topic of pie-tin returning. Now say something else.* But she didn't.

He smiled with an almost-boyish bashfulness. "Actually, I thought maybe..."

The phone rang, and Eve held up a finger to

Dylan. He waited while she spoke with another real estate agent. She gave Dylan a helpless look as the call dragged out. When she was finally able to end it, she looked up at Dylan. "Sorry. What were you saying?"

He said, "I was thinking... if you weren't too busy..."

A message popped up on her computer screen with a ding. She glanced at it then did a double take. "Oh. That's not good. I'm so sorry. Just give me a second." She quickly typed a message, sent it, then looked up at Dylan. "I'm really sorry. I can go for an hour with no interruptions, and then this happens. I'm so sorry. Again. You were saying?"

"I was thinking you looked really busy. We'll catch up some other time." With a wave, he walked out the door.

Caroline rushed down the stairs. "What just happened?"

"Dylan left."

"I know that, but what happened?"

"I'm not sure. It almost sounded like he was going to ask me out. But I guess he changed his mind and left."

"Why?"

"I don't know. Because I'm repulsive?"

Caroline started to laugh. "No, I don't think that's the reason."

Eve glanced away as though it didn't matter, but she couldn't even convince herself. She shifted gears and tried to move on. "So, how was your conference call?"

"What conference call?"

"The one you went upstairs for. Remember?"

Caroline looked stunned, then her expression changed. "I went upstairs to give you and Dylan time alone."

"Alone... here at work?" Eve was completely perplexed.

Caroline stared as though Eve had just lost her mind. "He was trying to ask you out."

"Well, I thought maybe, but...?" *But what? Then he came to his senses? Realized his mistake?*

Caroline shook her head slowly. "Wow, the two of you. Yes, he just needed a little encouragement."

"From me? How was I supposed to know that?" Eve should've grown used to this feeling of being lost and out of sync. When she got pregnant with Lydia, life had become a series of situations in which she didn't fit because she hadn't followed the usual path. And now, here she was, a thirty-five-year-old adolescent.

Caroline sat down on the bottom step. "It's okay. I guess while the rest of us were learning the secret unwritten code of romantic relationships, you were busy changing diapers, raising a child."

That was an understatement. Eve had learned to work beyond her uncomfortable shyness in practical matters, but dating was anything but practical. She had tried to date a few times, but after several failed attempts, she'd found it easier to shut off that part of her life and focus on her daughter. She'd never meant it to be permanent, but years had passed. Now, she'd just botched up her big chance to date Dylan, and the whole thing felt like torture.

Eve heaved a defeated sigh. "I really liked him."

"Liked? What, you don't like him anymore?"

"Well, yes, but he's gone."

Caroline smiled. "Oh, this isn't over."

"It's not?"

With a frank look, Caroline said, "Oh, no. Dylan's crazy about you. Can't you see that? Never mind. Don't answer that. Just trust me. He is." Caroline got that look on her face like when she was working out a real estate deal in her head. She took so long that Eve wasn't sure whether the conversation was over or not. Then Caroline's face lit up. "Eve, are you busy tonight?"

Thinking Caroline had moved on to thoughts about work, Eve said, "No, I guess I could work late if you need me."

"Work? Who said anything about work? You are going out on a date."

"Oh really? Who with?" *At least I'm not the only one here who's crazy. Caroline isn't making sense, either.*

Caroline picked up her phone. "Dylan, hi!" She flashed a smile at Eve. "No, the plumbing is just fine. It's just, I had a thought, and since you were just here, you came to mind first." Caroline nodded in response to something Dylan must've said. "I was hoping you'd do me a favor. I've got this gift card that's about to expire. I'm just buried in work, so I was hoping you might take it off my hands... No, no. I just don't have the time. It expires tonight, so if you don't use it, it'll go to waste. It's for dinner for two at Silva Brothers' Brewpub. Oh! Why don't you take Eve?" She smiled at Eve and started nodding. "Should she meet you there? Oh, wait, isn't her place on the way? That's what I thought. So what time can you be there?" Caroline was absolutely beaming. "Oh, right. I guess you would want to change out of your work clothes. Why don't you go home and get changed, and then you could pick Eve up on your way, say, eight o'clock?" Caroline did a fist pump. "Great. I'll tell her."

Eve stared, her jaw stuck open.

Caroline stood up. "Don't just sit there. Go home and get ready. You've got a date tonight! I'll call Silva Brothers' and make the arrangements."

Still feeling a little bit stunned, Eve pulled her purse from her bottom desk drawer and started to leave. "Oh, the gift card! I guess we'll need that."

Caroline's eyebrows drew together in confusion. "What gift card?"

"The one you said you had."

"There's no gift card, but I'll call and make sure they say that there's one."

Eve couldn't quite believe it. "You made the whole thing up?"

Caroline shrugged. "Yeah. What's your point?"

"Nothing. I just didn't think—"

"Of course not, because you have more important things to do, like get ready." Her eyes twinkled as she sternly shooed Eve from the house. "Go on. The clock's ticking!"

## CHAPTER NINE

On the drive home from Caroline's house, Eve tried not to think of the evening to come. It would only make her more nervous. As a result, that was all she could think about. She reminded herself that it wasn't a real date. Dylan had more or less been roped into going out with her. Still, it had broken the ice. Although breaking ice didn't always end well.

*Stop, Eve. Think positively. This will give us a chance to talk.* That was a good thing, regardless of the direction their relationship took. Seeing Dylan again had been a reminder of the most difficult time in her life. It was time she came to terms with the past.

Looking back, she could see things more clearly, especially where Dylan was concerned. The fact that he bore no hard feelings toward her only served to emphasize what a nice guy he was. At a time when Eve's world was imploding, Dylan had tried to do the right thing. The problem was, it wasn't his right thing to do. He'd been so heroic to step up and make such an offer, knowing what people would think. Their small town would've stayed busy with that bit of gossip for months. She'd told him she was sorry, and she knew he'd forgiven her, but it didn't seem like nearly enough. She supposed it would take time for both of them to not only let go but also forget.

On the plus side, she was proud of her daughter and the life she had built. It was her single greatest achievement. Lydia had grown up. She was ready to build her own separate life now. It was time to give her daughter the space she needed to be independent. That meant it was time for Eve to be independent.

Maybe Dylan would be good for her. Back then, the timing was wrong. *Is the timing right now?* She couldn't deny it was different to see him again. In some ways, he was almost a stranger. He looked different, older and stronger.

Eve's thoughts strayed. Dylan clearly worked out or did something athletic. She recalled seeing him on the floor, looking under her sink, all stretched out and sinewy. She'd been surprised by her reaction. As adept as she had become at burying feelings like those, she couldn't escape her attraction to him. Having him working upstairs while she tried to work downstairs had forced her to think about him until her nerve endings went *zing* at the sound of his footsteps on her stairs. But what sent her over the edge was his kindness. But he'd always been that—quiet and deep. Why had it taken her so long to notice?

Once home, she told Lydia she was going out for the evening.

Lydia's face wrinkled in confusion. "Going out?" She chuckled. "Mom, watch how you phrase things. That almost sounded like a date."

Eve felt a little indignant. "Well, it is, as a matter of fact."

"What?" Lydia looked at her as though she'd just dyed her hair green. Green hair might have been lovely on one of Lydia's friends, but it was clear from her horrified expression that neither green hair nor dates should be options for her mother.

"It's okay. I'm a grown-up. We're allowed."

Lydia looked as though she were the parent. "Technically, maybe, but... yeah, no."

Eve wasn't sure whether to laugh or be annoyed. She chose to smile, although it wasn't entirely sincere. "Okay, well, phew! Glad I don't have to ask your permission."

"But you haven't been on a date ever—or at least since I've known you, which is my whole life. Eighteen years. Do you even know what to do?"

Eve gave her the best smirk she could muster. "I'll figure it out." But in truth, she was stunned by the reminder. *When* was *the last date I went on?* Then she remembered. She remembered it well, in fact. That was the date when, halfway through dinner, she'd decided she would rather curl up with a book than her date—or any date, for that matter. That revelation was followed by a half hour of nodding politely as mind-numbing drivel spewed out of the mouth of a deceptively pleasant-looking young man.

Walking inside and closing the door at home, she'd said, "Never again," and gone to check on her three-year-old daughter. *Oh, crap. Fifteen years!* She redid the math. *Wow. Fifteen years living the life of a nun—if nuns had children and raised them alone.*

On the plus side, she had rendered Lydia speechless and staring as though her eyebrow muscles were getting a serious workout. Eve would have preferred an encouraging look that said, "Go out and have a good time, Mom!" But she counted her blessings. At least Lydia wasn't saying what she really thought.

Finally recovered from the initial horror of her mom going out on a date, Lydia grew deeply serious. "Mom, you've got to be careful of those dating apps. Although maybe the ones for seniors aren't quite so bad."

"Seniors? I'm thirty-six."

Unfazed, Lydia said, "The old guys on your app are probably nicer."

Eve laughed. "I didn't use an app."

Now her daughter looked worried. "Mom, you can't just go out with random people you meet!"

Eve nodded. "Yeah, I guess you're right."

"Of course I'm right!"

"Although Dylan isn't exactly random."

"Dylan?"

"Yes."

"The plumber?"

A glance at her watch sent Eve into warp speed. "Gotta go!"

A stunned Lydia still stood in the hall while Eve closed her bedroom door. Twenty minutes and three outfits later, she opened her door, looking pulled together and poised, which was no small feat. She ducked back for one last look in the mirror and declared herself ready to face the evening ahead. She emerged from her room to find Lydia waiting at the kitchen table with a can of soda in hand.

"How do I look?" Eve wasn't sure she wanted to hear the answer.

"You look great."

Eve made a face, and Lydia laughed. Then the doorbell rang. "He's downstairs." She bared her teeth in panic.

Lydia laughed. "Go on. You two kids go have fun."

Eve scowled and headed for the door.

Lydia called out, "Don't forget to use condoms!"

Eve's jaw dropped as she turned.

Lydia nearly did a spit take as she saw her mom's reaction. Unable to speak through her laughter, she set down her soda and waved her mom off.

Eve paused at the top of the stairs, took a few calming breaths, then went down to greet Dylan. She swung open the door and forgot all about how she looked or felt. All she saw was Dylan. "Hi."

He smiled. "Hi."

She'd grown used to seeing him in his work clothes, which looked really good on him. But this was different. He wasn't too dressed up. He was just wearing a sweater and jeans. But his hair was all neat. He was clean-shaven. But more than any of that, there was something in his eyes that she couldn't define.

"You look pretty." Three words. She hadn't heard those words from a man in so long. Had she ever heard those words?

"Thank you." She tried not to smile too much. *He was being polite. Don't get carried away. Be serene. It's just dinner. You're fine.* But when she lifted her eyes to meet his, she saw the same light she thought must be coming from hers. She couldn't be imagining that.

Minutes later, Theo seated them at the best table Silva Brothers' had. Located next to the window, it looked out over the dock to the harbor, where the water reflected the lights from the waterside buildings with a magical glimmer. As many times as Eve had been to the bar, it felt different, special, this time. Votive candles in holders shaped like pumpkins cast a warm glow over the table, while a fire crackled from the wood-burning stove in the corner. The gentle murmurs of scattered voices blended together, lending privacy to Eve and Dylan's conversation. Neither of them talked very much. Eve wondered how two people who tended toward shyness would fare on an evening out like this together. But it felt comfortable. Away from work, with no pressing appointments or tasks to be done, they could indulge in quiet contentment with nothing to do but be with each other.

"I have a confession." Dylan looked down and smiled bashfully. Something about it made her feel like they were okay together. "I've been wanting to ask you out pretty much since the first time I saw you again."

Eve wasn't sure whether to smile or act nonchalant, but she wasn't wired for nonchalant, so she lost herself in his gentle gray eyes.

Dylan continued. "I was going to ask you out earlier today, but I couldn't seem to get the words out. When I'm with you, I get a little tongue-tied."

He did that bashful smile again, which so disarmed her, Eve thought she might melt. "I get the same way."

"In general, or just around me?"

For some reason, Eve told the truth. "Around you."

Dylan exhaled with exaggerated relief. "Well, that's good."

"Is it? How so?"

"If we both feel the same, that makes us equally hopeless." He laughed.

"We're a perfect match."

His smile faded. "I was just thinking that."

Eve realized she'd stopped worrying what he would think about each thing she said or did. She didn't understand how he did it, but he put her at ease. "I wasn't sure what to expect this evening."

"How's it going so far?" Behind his smile, a hint of apprehension troubled his eyes.

Eve leaned forward. "Oh, nothing but good on your part, but I haven't really dated much over the years. I don't want to be awkward about it."

He reached out and put his hand on hers with a look that seemed to say it was okay. And it was. She could only recall a few times in life when she'd felt completely at peace. In that one moment, everything felt in balance, and she had the overwhelming sense that they would be okay. She could not have described it to anyone else, but it was as though she knew in her soul that they belonged together. It was too soon to say it out loud, but she knew it was real.

Their entrée came. Dylan slid his hand from hers, and the moment was gone.

After dinner, Dylan said, "I have a little surprise. It's not huge. Don't get your hopes up. But I thought you might enjoy it."

Theo stopped by the table and reminded them that the gift card had covered their dinner.

*A gift card named Caroline.* Eve resolved to do something extra special this week to thank her.

# CHAPTER TEN

Dylan left a generous tip on the table, then he explained where they were going as they walked to his car. Eve had half expected him to drive her around in his plumbing truck, but he'd picked her up in a red SUV. "There's an orchard a couple of towns over that does a harvest moon hayride. It's strictly for grown-ups."

"I've never been on a hayride at night. That sounds r—" She almost said "romantic." "Really nice."

Hearing her hesitation, Dylan glanced over at her but quickly returned his attention to the road.

At the orchard, they climbed onto the wagon and took their seats on the bales of hay lining the sides. The driver gave each couple a blanket, which Dylan dutifully wrapped around both their laps. While the driver served cups of hot mulled cider, he entertained everyone with harvest moon legends and superstitions.

"How many of you folks looked over your right shoulder at the harvest moon this evening?"

Judging by a few raised hands, Eve suspected they knew something she didn't. He continued, "Well, it's too late for this year. You have to do it the first time you see it, or it doesn't count. But if you do it next year, they say it brings luck."

Someone said, "Right shoulder? What if I'm left-handed?"

The driver said, "Then you have my sympathy."

Eve asked Dylan, "Did you see the moon over your right shoulder?"

He shook his head. "But I'm here with you, so I'm lucky already."

"Very smooth." Eve smiled, then she lowered her eyes, barely believing what was happening. If she'd known a date could feel like this, she would have gone on them early and often.

Once he had made sure everyone had enough blankets and cider, the driver hopped off the wagon to head for the tractor. "Before I go, I've got one more important bit of harvest moon wisdom for later this evening. When you go to bed tonight, remember this. Do not let the moon shine on your face while you sleep." He widened his eyes for an ominous look and said dramatically, "It's said to be dangerous." He nodded for emphasis. "And if you get moonshine on your face while you're awake, you've probably had too much to drink."

With that, the hayride began. The wagon

wheels crunched over the gravel and leaves that were beginning to blanket the dirt road. A few couples talked quietly, but Eve and Dylan sipped their hot cider and took in the view. The rolling hills were a patchwork of orchards, crops, and rows of plowed-over farmland.

Eve drew in a deep breath. "You can smell autumn in the air—fallen leaves, bales of hay, and hot cider."

Dylan didn't say anything, but the warmth in his eyes was enough. As he put his arm about Eve's shoulders and drew her against him, he said, "It's good."

For Eve, it was better than good. It was perfect.

The faint scent of a bonfire wafted through the air and signaled they were nearly back to the main building. Snuggled close to a man she was starting to care for, Eve was reluctant to see the ride end. His warm breath brushed her cheek, and she wanted to lift her chin until her lips met his, but the wagon pulled to a stop. The ride ended. The chill of the night air rushed between them as they parted. Dylan hopped down from the wagon and steadied Eve's hand as she stepped down to the ground. He held her hand as they walked to his car. Everything felt so easy with Dylan.

*So, this is happiness.*

Eleven o'clock was still early, as dates went—or at least it felt early to Eve. So she did something she had never done before. She invited Dylan in for some coffee. Lydia's parting words about condoms echoed inside her head, so she tried to clarify matters, lest Dylan think she meant more than just coffee. "Lydia will be there as our chaperone." She made a feeble attempt at a laugh.

With a gentle smile, Dylan said, "Coffee sounds good."

Without the magic of dim restaurant lighting or harvest moonglow, they sat on Eve's sofa and talked. She made a mental note that she really needed to up her lighting game in the apartment. She had decorated with only Lydia and herself in mind, so she was short on mood lighting.

Dylan didn't seem to mind. He looked around at the minimalist decor. It was simple and tasteful. "You've built a good life for yourself."

He didn't go so far as to say she had made the right choices. That was tactful of him. Eve wasn't sure herself that she'd chosen well, but life was like that. No one made all the right choices—no one she knew, anyway. "Things have a way of working out no matter what choices we make. I did the best I knew how."

"Lydia's amazing."

"Thanks. I'm proud of her. Hailey's so sweet."

With a nod, Dylan said, "As you said, things have a way of working out. The marriage was a mistake, but Hailey was not. That's the one thing that has gotten us through the divorce and why we're still able to talk to each other. We both love Hailey."

His words brought Jack to mind. Lydia's father was someone she'd managed to leave in the past, for the most part. "Sometimes I wonder if I made a mistake by not telling her father." With some reluctance, she looked Dylan in the eye.

"Jack?" The look on his face told her there was no point in trying to hide it. "He knew."

"I guess I knew deep down that he didn't care, so I never told him. Maybe it was selfish, but I couldn't bear the reminder of how little it all meant to him. So I just closed that door and moved on with my life." She turned to him, but he wouldn't meet her eyes. "But you told him. When did you know?"

"In school once, you rushed out of the room in the middle of class, and I followed you."

"Yeah, I think I remember that. But I told you I had the flu."

"A teenage girl doesn't get the flu every morning." He looked at her then, and she felt the same sinking feeling she'd felt back then.

Eve looked away. "You shouldn't have told him."

"I didn't at first, but I couldn't watch you suffer alone day after day."

"I thought I was hiding it. How did you know?"

"Eve." He touched her chin and gently guided

it toward him until she looked into his eyes. "I knew."

She wanted to run, but she couldn't run away from the past or her feelings for Dylan. It was too late. Too many emotions were tangled between them.

He lowered his hand and looked away. "Jack just went on with his life as though nothing had happened—as though *you* hadn't happened. He made me sick. So I told him. I thought I'd force him to man up."

"But he didn't." Eve thought she'd processed all the old feelings and boxed and stored them away. She was wrong.

"We fought. It didn't do any good."

"I didn't know." Eve felt as though the wind had been knocked out of her.

"So if he wouldn't make it right, I decided I would."

After years of wanting to say it, she struggled for words. "I didn't handle that well. I was horrible to you."

"I was young and naïve. I thought I could fix things."

"I love that you tried." She'd often wondered why the moments in her life that required the most wisdom seemed to occur when she had the least.

He ran his hand over his hair. "I don't think you did then. I know I made matters worse, and I'm sorry about that. You had enough going on without having me ride in on my white horse and disrupt everything further."

She smiled. "I still like the idea of white horses, and what you did was heroic."

"If being an idiot is heroic." He laughed.

"No one ever tried to rescue me before or since. I didn't know at the time what I wanted or needed, but I came to appreciate the gesture."

He looked down with that bashful look Eve found so endearing. "It was more than a gesture." He hesitated as if measuring his words. "To be honest, it was selfish. I wanted to marry you. I may have been young and idealistic, but I knew that I cared for you." He hesitated to continue. "And I still do."

When she was able to meet his gaze, it was almost too much to take in.

He looked up and gave his head a slight shake. "There, I've done it again—gone and said it out loud."

He got half of "I'm sorry" out before Eve leaned over and kissed him. It was a bold move done without thinking.

"I'm sorry. I've never done that before."

"Well, you should." His eyes twinkled. "Often. Starting now." Dylan swept Eve into his arms and kissed her until she felt dizzy from the tsunami of emotions destroying every wall she'd protected her heart with. And she didn't care. Caught up in the thrill of their emotional connection, Eve could have gone on kissing Dylan all night, but he pulled back and held her shoulders. "I... had better leave."

The sudden sense of abandonment caught Eve off guard.

"Don't get me wrong. I'd love to stay, but I need to go now, or I won't." He gave her hand a squeeze then stood.

Eve followed him to the door. Once there, he took her face in his hands and touched his lips to hers softly. No matter how light the kiss, its effect was powerful. Eve had followed one evening of reckless abandon with eighteen years of holding her emotions in check. Now, in one evening, she'd thrown open the floodgates. *What am I doing?*

His lips brushed hers as he whispered, "Good night, Eve Parker."

"Good night." Her voice barely made a sound.

After one more lingering gaze, Dylan turned and put his hand on the doorknob. But he suddenly swiveled back to her and pulled her into a knee-buckling kiss. She might have grasped for something to steady herself, but he had his arms firmly about her. Evidently, the human heart could endure overpowering bliss, because she was still breathing, albeit unevenly, when that kiss ended. His eyes swept over her face, then abruptly, he planted a kiss on her forehead and left without a word.

*What am I doing? I'm falling in love.*

# CHAPTER ELEVEN

Tears trickled down Lydia's face as she sat on her bed with her back to the wall. She had never meant to eavesdrop. But the walls were thin, and she couldn't help it. She would give anything not to have heard. Her mother had always been vague about her father, to the point that Lydia had stopped asking about him. She had pieced together her own version of what must have happened, and she had come to terms with it. She was even okay with not having a father since she had never had one. Despite the occasional school event when she would see other kids with their fathers and wonder what it would be like, for the most part, it wasn't an issue. What she was not okay with was hearing her mother and Dylan discuss her father, not only by name but with the understanding that Dylan knew the full story—a story Lydia had never been told.

Jack. So that was his name. Her father was Jack. All of these years, her mother had known who he was yet withheld that information from her daughter, the one person who had a right to know it. Why? Was he some kind of horrible monster? If so, what did that say about Lydia?

If her mother wouldn't tell her, then, armed with his name, she would find out the rest on her own. She waited until her mother had gone to bed. It was quiet. She waited another half hour after that. Then she crept into the living room and retrieved her mother's high school yearbooks from their neglected spot on the bottom bookshelf. There were two other Jacks in the yearbook, but one, in particular, seemed to appear beside Dylan a number of times.

Dylan hadn't changed all that much. His hair was longer back then, but there was no mistaking that face. The Jack in the picture had to be her father. Jack Watkins, quarterback of the football team, also played on the baseball and basketball teams. *Busy guy. Quite the athlete.* In that regard, Lydia clearly took after her mother. Genetics were weird. What had she inherited from Jack? His family might have a genetic predisposition to some disease that struck everyone at the age of eighteen. Things like that would be good to know. But she had been denied that sort of vital information. Worse, she had been denied a father.

Where was he now? Some people moved away to big cities, remote cabins, or even across the country. Was Jack one of those people? She had so many questions. Lydia crept back into the living room and returned the yearbooks, then she went back to her room and fell asleep on her tear-moistened pillow.

"Leave me alone," Lydia muttered as she reached for her phone.

Marco had texted her: *Can you proofread this paper I wrote? I've got to work all weekend. So I need to have it finished and ready for school on Monday.*

Lydia stared at the screen. With little thought, she quickly dashed off an answer. *Sorry, I can't. My life is over.*

She stuck her phone under the pillow and cried. She could still hear the phone chime. She ignored it. But fifteen minutes later, she couldn't ignore the sound of pieces of gravel hitting her window every few seconds. It was relentless.

*One o'clock in the morning?* It was probably some mischievous kids wandering the quiet harbor area. They were probably only a couple of years younger than she was, which made her feel old and weary.

The stones stopped. *Got bored and moved on? Good. Losers.* She adjusted her pillow and closed her eyes, hoping for sleep.

Louder tapping on the window dashed those hopes. "Lydia!"

She knew that voice. *You have got to be kidding. Your paper? Now?*

"Lydia! It's Marco." He was halfway up, deftly climbing the tree, by the time she reached the window.

"Marco! What the heck are you doing?" For a fleeting moment, she seemed to recall having a fantasy similar to this, but it had taken a wrong turn on its way to reality.

"Could you open the window a little bit more?"

Lydia was too baffled to form words, but she did as he asked. His transfer from the tree to her window was tricky. She couldn't stand by and risk watching him fall, so she grabbed an arm and pulled him inside the rest of the way. It was a matter of safety. But she didn't expect what happened next—not that she'd never wondered what it might be like to have him on top of her. He was the sort of guy who could make a mind wander in that direction. She just hadn't expected, in doing so, he would knock the wind out of her. She lay pinned to the floor, unable to draw in a breath. Marco looked down at her for a moment. It felt more like a few dozen moments, but he came to his senses and rolled off to the side.

Apparently realizing what was the matter—the fact that she wasn't breathing was a pretty good clue—Marco lifted her knees, hoisting her up to a semi-sitting position, and supported her from behind. He put his arms around her. "Breathe in through your nose and out through your mouth."

*Can't breathe. At all.*

"You can do it."

To her surprise, she began breathing again.

"That's it. Relax. Just breathe."

*Crap. Not breathing really ruined that moment.* Once she resumed breathing easily, she remembered why she felt wrung out emotionally —and that she didn't want to help Marco with his paper. Sure, she liked him. She liked him a lot. But she also knew where she stood with him. Helping him with his papers wouldn't change that.

But then he tightened his arms around her and held her against him. Face-to-face would have been better, but she was in no position to argue.

He pressed his cheek against her head as he held her—something he was very good at, she had to admit. "Are you okay?"

She frowned. "Yeah. I can breathe now."

"Thank God. You had me so worried."

Was this really the time to tell him he might be overreacting a little? It wouldn't hurt to let him hold her a little bit longer—if it made him feel better. "I just had the wind knocked out of me. I'm fine now." *Ugh. I really wish I hadn't had to say that.*

He leaned back, rubbed her shoulders, then scrambled around so he faced her. Thank God she hadn't seen that look in his eyes while he was holding her, or she might have swooned. More than once, she'd made a note of the soft look in his deep-set brown eyes, but she'd never had its all-encompassing power focused fully on her.

She still wasn't quite sure this wasn't a dream, except she never had dreams this good. Marco made a pretty hot Romeo climbing up to her balcony. Although if she had designed the costumes for this dream, she would have gone full-on Elizabethan, codpiece and all. But jeans were good too.

No, this was no dream. This was Marco, which made it weird... and brought her back to her original question. "What are you doing here?"

His face lost all of its expression and some of its color. "Your text."

Picking up on her confusion, he repeated verbatim. "'Sorry, I can't. My life is over.'"

*What is your problem?* Then she realized what must have happened. "Oh! Oh, wow. You thought I was going to..."

"Yes! Because you said as much!"

"Marco, I am so sorry!"

"Look, no matter what's going on, we can get through it."

*We? When did we become a we?* "Marco, I'm fine."

"You don't have to say that. It's me. You can talk to me. Let me help."

He really thought she was thinking of ending her life. "Marco, no. Really, I'm fine."

"Yeah, I could tell by your text."

There was a knock on her door. "Lydia, are you okay?"

Lydia's eyes widened. Marco was in her bedroom, and her mother was on the other side of the door. There was no good ending to this if her mother walked in. "I'm fine, Mom. I was just... listening to a podcast."

"Oh, okay. Turn it down. Get some sleep."

"Okay. Night." She held a finger to her lips as if Marco needed to be told to be quiet. This didn't look any better for him than for her.

Lydia listened for the familiar sounds—a closed door followed by the squeak of the springs as her mother went back to bed. Then she quietly whispered, "So you came all the way here to save me?"

He smirked. "Well, yeah. Why wouldn't I? I was afraid I wouldn't get here in time."

She could think of so many reasons, but the fact that he cared touched her deeply. "So you climbed that tree?"

He lifted his shoulders.

*You did that for me?* "Thank you. I'm sorry it was a false alarm."

"Really? I'm glad it was."

"But I would never mislead you like that—about something that big. I had a friend who tried to kill herself once. It was awful and sad."

"Oh man. Did she get help?"

"Yeah, she was one of the lucky ones. Her parents had no clue. None of us did. But they took her to several therapists and psychiatrists until they found the right people who could help her with the right medication and therapy."

"So she's better now?"

"Yeah, for the most part. She still struggles with bouts of depression, but now she knows she doesn't have to suffer alone. She's always a phone call away from help. She showed me a piece of paper she keeps in her wallet. 'The bad days don't last forever.'"

"Good words to remember."

This was a new side of Marco. He almost seemed thoughtful and serious. Then he proved it by turning his attention to Lydia. "What about you? Something's wrong. I can tell."

"Yeah."

"So?"

"So my mother and Dylan were in the next room."

"Your mother and Dylan?"

As if smirking weren't enough, she added an eye roll. "They went out on a date. And I overheard them—"

"You heard them?" His eyebrows shot up. "They didn't... They weren't... Were they?"

Lydia gasped. "Ew! No!" She shuddered. She needed a moment to get back on track. "No, they were talking."

Marco lifted an eyebrow. "That must have been some conversation."

"It was." Lydia went through what she'd heard

and finished with, "So, short version—I've got a father, and my mother lied about it."

"I think I know a little of how you must feel. I lost my parents, and you lost your father before you ever knew him. I know it's not the same, but either way, I know that feeling—like something's missing."

Lydia lifted her chin, almost nodding, then stared at the wall.

"Hey. Come here." Marco put his arm around her shoulders. "What are you thinking?"

"Nothing. No, actually, I'm thinking you're right. Something's missing, but I don't even know what it is—or who he is."

He leaned his head on hers, and she settled into the crook of his neck. For a while, they sat in silence, side by side on the floor at the foot of her bed, with their backs against the foot of the mattress.

Lydia sighed. "I just want to know."

Marco lifted his chin. "I'd like to know what kind of father would ignore his daughter for eighteen years."

Lydia didn't have an answer for that. "I don't know. I just want to see him."

"What are you going to do?"

Lydia shook her head. "I don't even know where he is. All I've got is a name." She glanced over at her laptop. "I tried to find where he is, but the trail goes cold after high school. I was going to try one of those online people searches, but I don't have a credit card."

"Is that all?" Marco reached into his pocket and pulled out his wallet. "Here, use mine."

"I couldn't."

"Why not? I've got money in there I haven't even spent yet." He gave her a look as if not using it would be wrong. "Take it."

"Really?" She considered it for a moment then said, "I'll pay you back."

"I know you will—by reading my paper."

Infused with the sudden power of possibilities, Lydia grabbed her laptop and got to work. Minutes later, she had what they needed. Jack Watkins had a car dealership in Bangor.

"That's not too far away. I could drive it," she said then realized one huge flaw in her plan. "If I had a car." She turned slowly to Marco.

## CHAPTER TWELVE

Eve spent a leisurely morning sipping coffee and revisiting her evening with Dylan—every word, every gesture. How had she failed to notice what a great guy he was in high school? She chalked it up to being young and foolish.

By noon, she began to wonder about Lydia. The girl was a power sleeper, but it was noon. Not even Lydia could sleep later than that. Eve went to Lydia's door and tapped lightly. When she got no answer, she knocked. After a louder knock, Eve grew concerned. "Lydia? Mind if I come in?" When she got no answer, she opened the door a crack. "Lydia?"

There was a note on the bed. It began with "Don't worry." Immediately, Eve worried. "I've gone to see Jack."

*Jack?* Eve's heart sank. *How could she know?* Then she felt sick to her stomach. Lydia must have heard her talking with Dylan. Given the timing, that had to be it. She and Dylan hadn't been talking loudly, but they had been loud enough. Somehow, her daughter had managed to piece together Jack's full name and address. That was a mystery she would have to solve later. Right now, she had to do something. Too panicked to think clearly, Eve knew she had to go to her daughter, but she had no idea where that might be.

Jack had left Pine Harbor right after high school. She had to figure out who, after all these years, might have kept in touch with him enough to know where he was now. If anyone knew, it would be Dylan—the last person she wanted to involve in this mess. But Lydia was her daughter, and Eve would move mountains to keep her child safe. Nothing else mattered. She had to find Lydia.

Eve pulled herself together. She didn't have time to indulge in emotions right now. If she had learned anything over the years, it was how to shut off her feelings and get the job done. So she picked up her phone and called Dylan.

He arrived at her door surprisingly quickly—in less time than it should've taken him while driving the speed limit. She was waiting for him downstairs by the door. Dylan unlocked his car door and rolled down the window. "Get in. Fill me in on the way."

Buckling her seat belt, Eve said, "She's not answering her phone. I've texted and called."

"If you were Lydia right now, would you?"

"No, because I'd know what was waiting on the other end."

With a tender smile, Dylan took the edge off Eve's frustration.

She shut her eyes for a moment. "I'm sorry."

Dylan shook his head. "That's enough of that. Let's focus on finding Lydia and bringing her home."

Eve nodded and tamped down her frantic desperation.

Dylan squeezed her hand. "Why don't you tell me what happened?"

"There's not much to tell. She left a note saying she was with Marco. He drove her to see Jack."

"That's good."

"Is it? That wasn't my first thought."

"Marco might be a bit of a flirt—"

Eve's jaw dropped, but before she could speak, Dylan said, "But he's smart, and he's strong. He'll take care of her."

"Good. And then I'll take care of him." *So much for tamping down my emotions.*

Dylan put his hand on the back of her neck. It helped ease some of her tension, but the guy wasn't a miracle worker. Eve forced her thoughts back to the task at hand. There would be plenty of time to panic later. It wouldn't be wasted. She was storing it up. It occurred to her that she had no idea where they were going, but Dylan seemed to. "I take it you know where he lives."

"No, but I know where he works. We haven't been in touch since high school, but Dad keeps me posted. You know how he is. He loves to talk, and people love to talk to him. Apparently, Jack owns a car dealership up near Bangor. It shouldn't be too hard to find."

She stared out the window without noticing anything that she saw. "You don't think he would hurt her, do you?"

"Emotionally, maybe. Jack might've been a self-centered, womanizing jerk, but he wasn't intentionally cruel or violent. The Jack I knew wouldn't hurt her."

"Well, let's hope he's still the Jack we knew in high school. But people change."

Dylan stared at the road. "I'm sorry he hurt you."

Eve almost smiled. "You know, he did hurt me. And I can't lie. The pregnancy was awful. I was sick all the time. I was scared. My parents were angry at first, and then they were so disappointed. I wanted to crawl into bed and never get up again. But then after all of the pain, I held Lydia in my arms and was overwhelmed by love. You know. You have a daughter."

His eyes may have stayed on the road, but they were shining. "I do."

"For me, that was it. I didn't care about Jack. I did my best to erase him. All that mattered was my baby. She was mine, and I loved her. And I felt something I hadn't felt in months. I felt hope."

Dylan drove on without saying more, and yet somehow, just being with him gave her comfort. He was silent and strong—a rock she could lean on if she let herself. She didn't have very much practice leaning on people, and she hoped she wouldn't need to today. But there was something almost soothing about knowing she could because Dylan was there. He was there for her. She would never forget this. She wanted to tell him how grateful she was, but trying to tell him would only open the floodgates. As much as they had been through together, not even Dylan was ready to experience Eve's version of an ugly cry.

Dylan broke the silence. "On the plus side, she left you a note."

Eve exhaled and lifted an eyebrow. "Notwithstanding today, she's actually pretty levelheaded. And since it's only the two of us, we keep pretty close tabs on each other. Which means she knows what she's putting me through. So after I find that she's safe, I'll hold her in my arms." Eve narrowed her eyes. "And then I'll have a few choice words for her."

Eve inhaled sharply. "Theo!" She pulled out her phone and dialed. "Theo?"

"Hi, Eve. What's up?"

She quickly said, "Well, for starters, your brother has run off with my daughter."

"What? Marco and Lydia? Eloped?"

"No, not like that. But she found out who her father is."

"I don't understand."

"Long story. Anyway, Marco's taking her to Bangor to see him."

"Eve, where are you? I'll be right there. Don't worry. We'll figure this out."

"Thanks, but I'm with Dylan. We're on our way to Bangor to find her—them."

"Okay. So what can I do? I mean, I'll obviously call him."

"Yes, please do! Oh—and Theo, could you text me his phone number?"

"Yes, absolutely."

"Great. I'll keep you posted. Thanks. Goodbye."

Eve's phone chimed with an incoming message. Theo had sent Marco's number. Eve called, but it went straight to voicemail. "I don't know what I expected. That he'd answer and we'd have a nice chat?" She let her head fall back against the headrest.

Dylan slipped his hand over hers.

Marco followed the long line of cars leading onto the field next to Jack's car dealership. He opened the window and paid the parking attendant. "I must be in the wrong place. I'm looking for the entrance to the car dealership."

She grinned. "Oh, you're in the right place. It's Jack's annual Jack-O'-Lantern Pumpkin Carving and Car Clearance Festival." Despite being a little bit stunned, Marco nodded politely as she explained. "You must not be from around here. It's our tenth year. It's become a tradition."

"Jack Watkins owns all this?"

"Ayuh. Everyone calls him Pumpkin Jack."

Under her breath, Lydia repeated, "Pumpkin Jack." While Marco followed the parking attendants waving wand flashlights to a parking space, Lydia stared at the spectacle. "This was a mistake."

"I wouldn't go that far, but our timing's a little off." He put the car in park and hopped out while Lydia pulled it together. With a sigh, she got out of the car to meet Marco. As he rounded the corner, he stopped abruptly and looked down at his feet. Slowly lifting his foot, he said, "Watch your step. This field has seen more cows than cars." After he'd wiped his shoe on some thick grass nearby, they proceeded to head for the car dealership.

PT Barnum had nothing on Pumpkin Jack. This guy could put on a circus. People wandered about in costumes while the local cheerleading squad, dressed as gourds, cartwheeled their way down a cordoned-off path.

While she watched a gourd land in a split, Lydia bumped into a walking ear of corn. "Excuse me."

"Aw, shucks," it said with a chuckle.

*This isn't happening.*

Marco studied her. "Are you okay?" Without waiting for an answer, he slipped his hand into hers and kept walking. They passed some trunk-or-treat cars, where bundled cornstalks, hay bales, and buckets of candy festooned the trunks.

"I should have checked the website first," she said, feeling overwhelmed.

To their left was the entrance to a corn maze, which a sign said was "corn-mazing." On checkered tablecloths, plastic cups filled with orange beer sat waiting for anyone who dared to drink six beers, put their forehead to a baseball bat, spin around ten times, then enter the maze.

Marco watched someone try. A good-natured or overserved gentleman beside Marco said, "You haven't lived till you've tried it. Anyone who gets out on their own wins a chance to win that vintage truck over there." "Vintage" was a generous term in this case. The big prize at stake was a very used truck painted pumpkin orange. Marco nodded. It was impressive, in its way. Then he tightened his grip on Lydia's hand and quickened the pace.

At a long row of tables to their right, there must have been at least thirty children armed with pumpkin-carving knives and fresh pumpkins, accompanied by determined parents with eyes on the prize—this time, a black subcompact with a broom sticking out of the trunk. Marco muttered, "What could possibly go wrong?"

Marco kept looking at Lydia with a worried expression. "Hang in there. We'll just find Jack, and then we'll be fine." He gazed at her with such tender concern. It would have made her knees weak any other day, but today, it wasn't enough.

It was all she could do to hold back her tears. "I've had nightmares more pleasant than this."

Marco stopped walking and peered into Lydia's eyes. "Hey. We got this." He nodded as though he believed it. One of them had to. She certainly didn't. What he did next was a testament to how bad she must've looked, because he just pulled her into his arms and gave her a quick hug and a kiss on the forehead.

For the past few minutes, they'd followed a path to a large orange hot-air balloon. Someone near them said, "There he is! There's Pumpkin Jack!" After the drive to Bangor and the walk through Pumpkin Jack's outdoor funhouse, there he was—Jack Watkins, her father.

She and Marco both recognized Jack at once. Lydia had taken phone pics of every yearbook shot he was in and had memorized them on the way over. His face looked a bit heavier, but it was hard to tell whether he'd put on any weight since he was dressed as a pumpkin. Despite that, he appeared tall and handsome—almost as good-looking as his yearbook photos.

He turned and climbed into the basket. Evidently, he and the scarecrow were getting ready to launch. Marco sprang into action, making his way through the crowd with Lydia in tow. The balloon lifted a foot off the ground then another.

Marco called out, "Jack!"

Her showman of a father flashed a grin toward the voice, then his gaze fell to Lydia. Their eyes locked. She couldn't move. She just watched him float away, staring at her.

# CHAPTER THIRTEEN

Rain pelted the windshield as Dylan and Eve reached the car dealership. A steady stream of cars headed out of the parking area, making it nearly impossible to pull onto the property. By the time they were able to park, the foot traffic had thinned out considerably. Ahead was an information booth, so they made that their first stop. The shutters were closed, but Eve heard voices inside. She knocked on a wooden shutter. It got quiet inside. No one answered, but Eve would not be deterred.

At last, a middle-aged man with a comb-over, wearing a short-sleeved button-down shirt, rounded the corner of the booth. "May I help you?" The three of them huddled beneath the overhang of the welcome booth's awning.

"We're looking for someone—Jack Watkins."

"You and everyone else. A nor'easter blew in. They said they had to land the balloon. But we haven't heard from them since."

"Balloon?" Eve was too tired for sleuthing. *Would someone just please tell me what's going on?*

"Yeah, everyone knew that a wicked bad storm was coming, but that's Jack..." He shook his head. "He's a daredevil. Won't take no for an answer."

"So he's lost?"

"No, he's around here somewhere. We all saw it go down. Must be a long walk. Or..." He leaned closer and spoke softly in confidence. "You might go check the beer tent."

They did, and they checked every building still open for Jack, Lydia, or Marco. They found someone who said he had seen Jack get into his car and drive off.

"Alone?" Eve asked.

The man chuckled. "Yeah, that might be a first."

Dylan thanked him, and they scoured the remaining cars in the parking area. It appeared as though Marco and Lydia were gone.

Rain-soaked and exhausted, Eve collapsed in the car seat and leaned her head back. She had voiced every question about where they might be. Now all that was left was to imagine every possible scenario—none of them good.

Eve's phone chimed. "It's a text from Theo. He says the kids are fine, but they were caught in a blinding rain and pulled over to wait it out."

She texted: *Where?*

Theo: *I asked, but Marco didn't answer.*

Eve: *Of course not. Thanks, Theo.*

When her phone chimed again, she drew in a quick breath. "Lydia."

She read the message to Dylan. "Mom, I don't want you to worry. We pulled over to wait for the rain to let up. I'll see you back home. Don't be mad."

"Don't be mad? Okay, how 'bout frantic, distraught, frustrated—nauseous? But I guess I can leave mad off the list."

Dylan squeezed her hand while she shut her eyes and took several deep breaths.

"Take my phone. If I answer her now, I'll unload on her. This isn't the right time for that. I will save that for later." She glanced over at Dylan. "I yell better when I've had a good night's sleep."

Dylan coaxed a smile from Eve. "She's okay."

"Yeah, but I'm not."

It was late afternoon when they pulled into Eve's driveway. Lydia and Marco were seated together on the steps. Lydia looked up at her mom and said softly, "I forgot my keys."

"Serves you right. And Allie couldn't let you in because she's at Theo's helping him at the pub while you two went off on your adventure."

Dylan put a gentle hand on Eve's shoulder. Her anger roiled to the surface. Even though she knew it would make matters worse, she couldn't hold it back any longer.

Lydia snapped back. "An adventure? You mean finding my father—the one you lied about?"

Dylan said, "Let's go inside."

Eve said quietly, "Thank you for everything, but I need to talk to my daughter alone."

She thought she detected some hurt in his eyes, but he said, "Of course." With a glance at Marco, he said, "Why don't you and I go to the pub? We can fill in your brother and Allie."

Marco didn't look thrilled at the prospect, but he didn't object. He just touched Lydia's hand then left. While Marco headed for his car, Dylan gave Eve a kiss on the cheek then headed for his.

Without a word, Eve and Lydia went inside and climbed the stairs to their apartment.

Silva Brothers' Brewpub had calmed down from the lunch rush and was preparing for dinner when Theo walked into the kitchen and nearly bumped into Allie on her way out. "Hold on."

Theo took Allie by the hand and led her to the far corner beside the walk-in cooler. "Come here, you." He circled his arms about her waist and planted a kiss on her lips. "Thank you. I couldn't have managed without you."

Her lips spread to a smile. "You could have, but thank you. I was happy to help."

With a glint in his eyes, he said, "You know what would make me happy?" He pulled her against him and buried his face in the side of her neck. "To lock the doors and go somewhere with you."

"Anyplace in particular?"

He raised an eyebrow. "Oh, I've got an idea or two."

She lifted her eyes. "I'm listening."

With a mischievous look, he gave his head a slight shake and leaned closer, lips parting.

The kitchen delivery door opened, and Marco walked in, followed by Dylan. Theo exhaled and gave Allie a look.

She put on a bright face. "I'll go refill the salt and pepper shakers on the tables."

In no mood for the discussion to follow, Theo glanced at Marco with cold eyes and went out to the bar.

Dylan followed and took a seat at the bar while Marco approached Theo. "I had to help her."

"And Allie had to give up her plans for the day to help me because you were gone."

Marco looked across the room at Allie then excused himself and went over to her. Theo was glad to see that Marco at least knew enough to apologize.

Dylan took a drink of his beer. "You look busy. Can I help?"

"No." Theo straightened and set down his cleaning rag. "But you could tell me what happened."

By the time Dylan finished, Marco was back helping his brother set up the bar for the evening.

Dylan said, "I hated dropping her off at home and leaving her there. I mean, Lydia was there, obviously, but Eve had a hell of a day, and I can't do anything to help her from here."

Although Theo appreciated Dylan's concern, he felt the need to point out, "Eve has been on her own for a number of years. She can manage."

"Oh, I know that. She's strong and independent—always has been. But after years of looking after Lydia, maybe it's time someone looked after her."

Theo eyed him for a moment. "And you think you're that someone?"

"I want to be." Dylan looked down into his beer.

"But?"

"I didn't say 'but.'"

"But you thought it."

Dylan averted his eyes from Theo's knowing look. "It's too early for buts."

Allie joined them and leaned on the edge of the bar. "Too early for what?"

Theo suppressed a grin then picked up on Dylan's apprehension. He imagined the last thing Dylan wanted was for Theo to bring one of Eve's friends into their conversation. Turning to Allie, Theo shifted the topic. "It's too early to go home and forget today happened."

Marco started to join them, but as he glanced from one to the other, he said, "I'll go wash the rest of the dishes."

When he was gone, Dylan said, "I wouldn't be too hard on him."

"Oh yeah? I can't think of a good reason not to." Theo's mouth quirked at the corner.

"Well, for one thing, I'm not sure if Eve sees it this way, but I was glad Marco was there. In her state of mind, Lydia didn't need to be wandering alone in a strange place. I think Marco probably knew how upset she was and did what was best and what was safest for her."

Theo took a moment to consider. "You're probably right. But now I'll have to tell him he did the right thing. Where's the fun in that?" He flashed a smile.

Dylan laughed.

Allie's jaw dropped. "Theo, that's terrible!" That only broadened Theo's smile. "The poor guy's in there, toiling away, driven by guilt, and you're just going to leave him that way?"

"Just till the dishes are done." Theo shrugged as though he were serious then suddenly laughed. "Come here." He put an arm around Allie. "I was on my way in to talk to him when you distracted me."

"Oh, right. Blame me."

"It's your own fault. You look so cute when you're outraged."

Allie looked at Dylan as if asking him what she should do with him. Dylan raised his palms in defense. "Leave me out of it. I'm just sitting here, drinking my beer."

Theo gave Allie a kiss on the forehead then went to the kitchen to talk to his brother.

Marco glanced up at Theo with dread.

Theo said, "You did the right thing."

"I know. I'm glad you figured it out. Look, here's what happened. She was going to get on a bus and head to Bangor—which she's never done. I couldn't let her do that."

"I know."

"So I gave her a ride because I'm not a jerk. End of story. I mean, what would you have done if it were Allie?"

Theo lifted an eyebrow. "But Allie's my girlfriend."

Marco dropped his guard for an instant—long enough for Theo to notice he'd touched a nerve. Marco quickly recovered. "And Lydia's my friend. Now, if you'll excuse me, I've got dishes and glasses to wash."

Marco pivoted and lifted a rack of dishes onto the dishwasher.

Theo grinned. "You like her." He didn't bother to pose it as a question.

"What?"

Theo wasn't fooled by Marco's wrinkled-up face. He could balk all he wanted. In fact, Marco's reaction confirmed his suspicions. Until now, Theo hadn't been able to figure out why Marco was different where Lydia was concerned. She was far from his type, so Theo had completely discounted the possibility of romance. But now it was so clear.

He nodded. "You like her."

"Screw the swear jar. That's bullshit!"

Theo tried to nod seriously, but erupting laughter betrayed him.

Marco lifted another dish rack. "Look, Theo, if you want to spin some sort of romantic fantasy in your head, have at it. Just don't bother me with your insane delusions."

Theo hadn't had this much fun in ages. "No, you're right. Nothing to look at here. You're just friends. Yeah, friends who ride to school together, study together, confide in each other, and travel together."

WHILE THEO HEADED into the kitchen to talk with his brother, Allie smiled to herself then said to Dylan, "It's none of my business, but..."

"Hold it right there."

"What?"

"Nothing good ever follows those words." He smiled and took a drink of his beer.

She put her hands on her hips. "I beg to differ." She leaned toward him. "It's none of my business, but... Eve likes you. If she pushes you away, just be patient."

"Nineteen years isn't patient?"

Allie looked straight into his eyes. "Oh, wow." *He's been in love with her since high school?*

Dylan looked frankly at her. "Yeah."

"Oh, Dylan. I didn't know."

Looking awkward, Dylan averted his eyes. "You don't need to tell her. I'm pretty sure she already knows. She just needs some space while she figures out what to do."

"We need to"—*lock you two in a room and not let you out until you come to your senses*—"do something to get her out of that apartment and get her mind off things. Hold on a minute." Allie went to the kitchen, where Marco had Theo in a playful headlock.

Marco released him and laughed. "Man, you are so lucky." He went out to the bar.

"Yeah, right." He grinned at Allie. "What's up?"

"What did you say to him?"

"The truth."

Allie thought about asking but chose to let it go. "Do you think it's too cold for the firepit?"

He walked over and drew her into his arms. "It's pretty chilly. We'll need to cuddle up close—for the heat."

She nodded. "That's what I'm thinking."

Theo leaned his forehead on hers. "Oh, sweetheart, I like how you think." He combed his fingers through her hair. "You know, in those chick flicks you watch, they always have to get naked—for the body heat. It's purely medical—to prevent hypothermia."

Allie barely suppressed her laughter. "Well, that's good to know, but I was thinking of Dylan."

Theo's eyes sparkled as he pretended to be confused. "You want to get naked with Dylan?"

Allie pushed him away. "No! What's the matter with you?"

Looking thoroughly entertained, Theo drew her back into his arms. "Just kidding."

Allie looked up and shook her head. "If I can get Eve over here, we could all go out after closing and sit around the firepit."

"You are..."

Anticipating his response, Allie exhaled, discouraged.

"Brilliant."

"Really?"

As if it were obvious, Theo said, "Yes! Those two are emotionally arrested at age sixteen—no, younger."

Allie agreed. "And they're crazy about each other. But without our help, I'm afraid they'll miss out on a second chance at love."

"Well, all right then. Let's do this."

They emerged from the kitchen to find Dylan standing, keys in hand. "Hey, thanks. I'm gonna go."

"No!" Realizing she'd practically shouted, Allie lowered her voice. "Stay for some dinner. How 'bout some chowder?"

"Thanks, but it's been quite a day. I just need to go home. I'm exhausted."

"Oh, okay." Allie hid her disappointment. As soon as the exit door closed behind Dylan, Allie and Theo turned to each other. In unison, they said, "Tomorrow."

## CHAPTER FOURTEEN

Lydia brought two cups of hot chocolate to the sofa and sat down cross-legged, facing her mother.

Eve wrapped her hands around the warm mug. "I like the service here."

Lydia said quietly, "Well, I owe you."

Eve held up her palm to stop her. "We've already hashed this all out. We've both made mistakes. Yours was worrying me, but I wouldn't have been so worried if I didn't love you so much. My mistake was far worse. We can't undo the past, but we can look to the future and try to avoid repeating our mistakes. I should have told you about Jack long ago. The thing is, I never made a conscious decision to keep it from you. You were too young at first. When you were old enough, Jack was gone. It was easier to leave him in the past. I couldn't see it from your point of view. I do now, and I'm sorry. I see how I hurt you."

Lydia stared abstractedly at the mug in her

hands. "I won't lie. I was angry at first, but when I calmed down and saw the big picture, I couldn't stay mad. You were in high school when you had me. I've thought about that a lot since I turned seventeen. I can't begin to imagine what you went through, so it's hard for me to judge you when I know I couldn't raise a child."

Bittersweet memories overwhelmed Eve for a moment. "Oh, sweetie, I've made so many mistakes. For the ones you're aware of, I guarantee there were so many more that you'll never know and I'll never remember. I just hope, when you look back on all that I've done wrong, you'll also remember how much I love you."

Lydia reached out, and they hugged. "I love you, too, Mommy."

She hadn't called Eve that since she turned thirteen. Something about that erased all the worry and guilt and brought them back into balance.

Lydia picked up her mug of hot chocolate. "Hugs and hot chocolate make everything better."

Eve smiled. "I couldn't agree more." Peace and contentment felt good after a difficult twenty-four hours, so they basked in it. Eve remembered holding a new baby in her arms as she sat with her mother, terrified she might make a mistake. Her mother had told her that as long as she loved her baby and made sure that she knew it, love would cover a multitude of sins. Eve had accused her mother of making stuff up to make her feel better. Her mother had said, "No, it's in the Bible, and you can't argue with God." She couldn't argue with her mother, either, so the matter was settled. She knew now that her mother had been right.

Eve finished her hot chocolate and leaned back, feeling tired but tranquil. Her mind wandered to less-frantic aspects of the day. She thought for a moment. "So, what's the deal with Marco?"

That killed Lydia's mood. "Mom! We're friends. Can't a girl have a friend who's a guy?"

"Of course." *Hmm. That was a little defensive. I wonder what that's all about.* Quickly changing the subject, she said, "I think we need some Jane Austen."

Lydia's face lit up as she hopped up and went to the movie cabinet. "I think I know just the one."

Eve headed for the kitchen. "I'll make some popcorn." They spent the rest of the evening curled up and sharing the opposite ends of a quilt, with a large bowl of popcorn between them.

THE TRIP to Bangor the previous day had caused Dylan to miss plans with his daughter. There was no school on that Monday, so Dylan took the day off from work and packed in a full day with Hailey, beginning with breakfast at her favorite fast-food burger joint. Then they hiked beneath a canopy of bright autumn leaves along one of the easier trails on the hills above Pine Harbor.

The leaves were in their prime, with rich red

and gold hues saturated by sunlight. After hiking, they topped the day off with some shopping, during which Haley didn't seem to notice what a fish out of water her father was as she shopped for jewelry at an accessory store. She was just happy to be with him, and that made him happy. After a picnic lunch by the water and an hour at an arcade, it was time to deliver her home to her mother. He pulled into the driveway and gave her a hug, then she ran up to the porch, where her mother waited. They offered one another a quick silent wave, the universal gesture of amicably divorced parents who tolerated one another for the sake of their children. Then he backed up the truck and headed off for an evening with Eve.

He and Eve had last-minute plans at Silva Brothers' with Theo and Allie. Dylan would have preferred an evening alone with Eve, but Theo had been very enthusiastic about having them over for dinner. He blamed it on Allie—something about the firepit and how it was their last chance to gather outside for the season. *We could gather inside,* he thought, but Dylan wasn't about to burst Allie's bubble. If the firepit meant so much to her, then they would go to the firepit. The truth was, he didn't care what he did as long as Eve did it with him.

After stopping by his place for a quick shower, Dylan headed over to Eve's. The firepit became more appealing as Dylan contemplated a brisk evening outside by a fire, sharing a blanket with

Eve. That would more than make up for the stress of the previous day.

As he pulled into the alley beside Eve's storefront apartment, a luxury car blocked his way. Caroline must have been showing high-ticket estates to one of her wealthy clients. Unable to pull through and park in the back where he usually did, he parked there. He and Eve would most likely be gone before anyone knew he was blocking their car. If by some chance they weren't, he would move. It wasn't his fault, after all. They were the ones who'd been thoughtless enough to block the alley.

His thoughts shifted to Eve, and he smiled as he rounded the corner. He did that a lot when he thought about Eve.

Then he stopped. "Jack." There they all sat, on the small shrub-lined deck in the back of the building. Eve, Lydia, and Jack stared at Dylan.

Jack stood, smiling, and stretched out his hand. "Dylan! How the hell are you? It's been years."

Dylan went through the motions of shaking Jack's hand. "I've been better."

Eve's eyes were acutely alert, a look she got when she was nervous.

*Good. If you're half as uncomfortable as I am, you deserve it. How could you entertain him as though he were part of the family?* But he was—biologically, anyway. It was Dylan who was the outsider. Of the four of them, Lydia had managed to look the most composed. Eve was tense, although Jack had no clue. He had one setting and one unrelenting expression—that grin. Dylan had gone through years of school with that grin staring him in the face, and all he could think of right now was the sheer joy of landing his fist in that grin.

"Lydia, why don't you and Jack go upstairs? There's some lemonade in the fridge."

With the enthusiasm of a large, lumbering hound, Jack said, "That sounds great. I'm parched."

While the two passed by on their way to the door, Eve hooked her arm around Dylan's with more tension than affection until they were gone. "Have a seat."

Dylan didn't want to have a seat. He didn't want to be here under these circumstances, and above all, he didn't want to be within miles of Jack. He couldn't escape the image of the happy little family who had greeted him with no warning mere moments before. Eve remained standing while Dylan paced the short length of the deck.

"He just showed up," she said. "We didn't know he was coming."

Dylan wasn't buying any of it. If it had anything to do with Jack, it was tainted. "He just showed up randomly on your doorstep?"

"No. Well, sort of. He came to see Lydia."

Dylan didn't know what to do with his anger. He didn't want to direct it at Lydia. She couldn't help what she'd been through or what she had done. It was understandable. But after the previous day, it was too soon. In fact, Jack was the last person Dylan cared to ever see.

Eve glanced toward the door and spoke quickly, clearly worried that they might return before she could finish. "He's kept tabs on us over the years."

"That doesn't sound creepy."

"I know how it sounds, but it wasn't. He happened to see us by chance, then he drove by a couple of times over the years."

Dylan raised an eyebrow.

"Look, Dylan, this isn't easy for me, either. How do you think I felt when I opened the door, and there he was? But my feelings don't matter—"

Dylan's temper flared as he gripped Eve's shoulders. "Your feelings do matter!"

With a level gaze, Eve said, "Not as much as my daughter's."

Dylan released her and walked to the edge of the deck. He stared out at the sea, the one constant in his life. "He'll break her heart."

"He might, but he's her father, and she wants to know him. It's her right, and it's her decision."

Dylan took a long while to swallow that bit of reasoning. Even if she was right, the whole thing felt wrong. He could barely unclench his jaw to get the next words out. "And what about you?"

"It's not about me."

The fact that Eve looked so resigned to the situation grated doubly on him. Then another thought sprang to mind and caught fire. Maybe there was another reason she was taking it so well. "You still have feelings for him."

"What?" She looked shocked, but protesting too much didn't always point to the truth.

"After all that he's done—or hasn't done—and after you've done all the work and raised Lydia on your own, he comes waltzing back into your lives. How convenient for him." In an instant, Dylan went beyond anger to numb disbelief. Devoid of emotion, he turned back to Eve. "And you let him."

The door swung open, and Jack ambled out to the deck, followed by Lydia, who carried a tray. "This lemonade hit the spot."

Jack leaned back as Dylan brushed past him and left. Behind him, he heard, "Same old Dylan. He's always been kind of moody."

Logs burned and crackled in the firepit behind Silva Brothers' Brewpub, sending sparks floating into the darkening sky as if on their way to join the stars. It was one of those nights when mild weather clung in a last-ditch attempt to keep winter at bay. But any Mainer knew that October snow could blow in any day, so they treasured the chance to sit outside together.

Kim and Caroline stopped by on their way to a jack-o'-lantern festival a few towns over.

Allie's face lit up. "Oh, that sounds amazing! I wish we'd thought of that."

With a knowing look, Kim folded her arms. "It's their annual singles night, in which anyone looks good standing next to a pumpkin, so I'm ready." Kim fluffed her hair and raised an eyebrow. "I've got great hopes. If it works out as planned, I'll be bringing home a hot guy tonight."

Caroline's eyes twinkled. "Me too—he'll be orange and round, and he'll be all aglow just because he's with me. And my lighter."

Seeing Dylan arrive all alone, Theo reached for a beer. "This one's got your name on it."

"Go ahead and put my name on a dozen more —make that a baker's dozen."

Theo pulled up a chair and offered it to Dylan. He took a breath and started to speak, but Dylan shook his head.

Kim eyed him for a moment. "How's—"

Allie interrupted, "The popcorn coming along? I don't know. Let's go check." Allie hooked elbows with Kim and dragged her back to the pub while Kim typed to the glow of her phone screen.

Caroline watched the whole scene but deftly filled the awkward silence that followed. "Don't you love the smell of the fire on these fall nights when the leaves swirl and crunch under your feet?"

"Speaking of feet, been on any good hikes lately?" Theo winced and shrugged at Caroline as if saying he was sorry. It was the best he could do.

If Dylan hadn't been in such a foul mood, Theo might have laughed at their feeble attempts to sidestep the elephant in the room—or on the beach. Not one person dared mention Eve's absence. Theo stumbled onward, firing questions at Dylan about his favorite hiking trails in the region. He knew that was one of Dylan's favorite topics. He was an avid hiker and had a lot of knowledge to share on the subject, but he barely registered a response.

Theo handed him another beer and looked up as Kim and Ally returned. "Where's the popcorn?"

For a second, Allie stared at him in confusion then recovered. "Oh, right, the popcorn. We're all out. Hey, Caroline, you're not getting away without a walk along the shore."

Caroline lifted her eyebrows. "Okay."

Allie pulled her up by the hands, and the three of them headed off on their walk.

Dylan said, "That didn't look too suspicious."

Theo wrinkled his face. "Yeah, subtlety isn't our strong suit. So, what's going on?"

Dylan rubbed his forehead. "What's going on? Jack." He glanced at Theo then shook his head. "Never mind. Let's just say Eve and I had a little discussion."

"When did this happen? I just saw you last night."

Dylan looked at his watch. "About an hour ago."

Theo couldn't believe it. He was clearly missing some facts, but if bartending had taught him anything, it was to read people's body language, and Dylan's said, "Leave me alone."

Theo did that for as long as he could, then he quietly said, "Sometimes talking helps."

Dylan took a swig of beer and shook Theo's hand. "Sorry, man. I just need to be alone."

"No worries. I get it." Theo clapped a hand on Dylan's shoulder and started to walk him back up to his car.

As the women returned from their walk, Kim tripped on a piece of driftwood. But she didn't let it slow her down. "Whoa! Hold on there! Where are you guys going?" Allie and Caroline caught up and stood by the firepit.

Dylan looked back. "I've got to go. You folks have fun."

"But the night is still young!" Allie nudged Kim to silence while Caroline shut her eyes for a moment.

"Yeah. You must be on your way soon to your fall festival."

Kim said, "Well, no, not necessarily."

Not even Caroline had the discretion to hide her disbelief. "What Kim means is that the event timing is flexible."

"Right!" Allie chimed in. "And we're having such a good time. Why cut it short?"

He eyed them suspiciously. "Whatever you're up to, the answer is no."

"No?" Kim looked as though she'd never heard the word.

With a friendly wave, Dylan said, "Thanks. Got to go."

Cars pulled in and out of the parking lot at the brewpub throughout the course of the evening, but when a familiar car pulled in past the main lot to the employee lot in the back, Dylan stopped in his tracks.

The car door slammed, and her shadowy figure headed down the footpath toward Dylan. He glanced back toward the firepit then stood his ground, facing Eve.

Kim and Caroline quietly said their goodbyes.

Allie said, "We'll walk you up to your car."

As they all passed Dylan and Eve, they said quiet goodbyes and left them alone.

# CHAPTER FIFTEEN

Allie looked out the window at the firepit, where Eve and Dylan appeared to be working things out—at least that was the plan, and she hoped it was working.

Theo joined her and slipped his hand in hers. "You sure know how to throw a party." He grinned.

Allie frowned. "Well, I tried."

"You and all of your friends. If those two don't get together, they have no one to blame but themselves."

She turned and walked with him to the bar. "I just want everyone happy, and Eve is long overdue for her share." She slid onto a barstool, and Theo stood beside her.

He took Allie's face in his hands. "You are a very good friend." He kissed her on the forehead and was on his way to her mouth when Marco paused opposite them at the bar. "Uh, excuse me, you two. Don't mind me. I'm just tending the bar."

With a glint in his eye, Theo said, "You're doing a fine job."

Marco shook his head. "Young love." Allie and Theo were instantly still, prompting Marco to look from one to the other. "Oh, oops. Too soon?"

Theo's eyes narrowed to a pointed glare.

Marco called out to Mel, who was bussing the last dinner table. "Hey, Mel, can you watch the bar for a minute? I have a sudden urge to go sort my socks in ROYGBIV order." No one else laughed, but that did nothing to tamp down Marco's amusement as he walked through the swinging doors to the kitchen.

Theo muttered, "Remind me why I keep him around."

"Because he's your brother."

"Oh, right. I knew there had to be a reason."

Quietly, Allie said, "Theo, it's fine."

"No, it's not." Theo glanced around.

Mel was at the other end of the bar, taking care of a handful of patrons. Marco was busy in the kitchen, doing anything he could to stay out of Theo's way. Theo knew Marco was kidding, but he'd stepped over the line.

He surprised Allie by leading her by the hand. "Theo? Where are we going?"

"Any place that's alone."

Allie had never seen Theo like this. He was angry and, apparently, trying to hold it in. That part wasn't going so well.

They went through the back door then

continued until Theo seemed satisfied no one would happen upon them. A lone string of lights surrounded the empty deck, shedding light on the bare decking below. The umbrellas and tables were gone, packed up for the winter, and the firepit glowed at the end of the path, by the water.

In the quiet night air, Allie replayed the past few minutes in her head, trying to pinpoint what had set Theo off. Marco had only been joking. She didn't mind being described as being in love. But with a sinking feeling, she realized love must be a sore subject for Theo. That didn't bode well.

Theo took Allie's hands. "I haven't been entirely truthful with you."

That didn't sound good. Here she'd been trying to fix everyone else's love life, only to find out something was terribly wrong with her own. "You're not married, are you?"

He leaned back. "What? No! Why would you think that?"

"Maybe because you're confessing to some deep, dark secret, and I'm trying to figure it out."

"Allie?" He searched her eyes, which was making it worse. "If my brother could figure it out, surely you can."

"Marco's very perceptive."

"Marco who? Because you cannot be talking about my brother. This is all his fault. This was not how I'd planned to tell you."

Allie braced herself.

Theo brushed some stray hair from his forehead. "Look, you can't say I didn't warn you. I did. I have wanted—and tried really hard—to give you some space and some time. Meeting someone on the day they're being proposed to doesn't exactly set things up for success. I knew you needed time, so I waited—and I was okay with waiting."

"Theo, what are you talking about?"

Theo groaned. "Well, I can't just have Marco dropping glib remarks and sit silently letting you think the wrong thing."

"Okay." She said it because it was something to say. In truth, she had no idea what he was talking about. And then it dawned on her. "Are you breaking up with me?"

"No! Allie—" He finished that thought with a kiss—a kiss heartfelt and passionate enough to convince her.

*Okay. If this isn't him breaking up, then what is it?* A scene from her past flashed in her memory. *Justin's proposal!* She measured her words. "Theo, I am so happy with where we are now, but I'm just not ready..." The crestfallen look on his face broke her heart. "I can see us going there someday, but it's only been—what? Four months? Marriage is a big step, and—"

"What? Marriage? What are you talking about?"

*Uh-oh.* "I don't know. What are *you* talking about?"

"Not marriage."

Allie winced. "Well, good. But then what's going on? I'm so confused."

"Love." Exasperated by the confusion, he blurted out, "I love you."

"Is that all?"

He looked cautious, at best, but nowhere near optimistic. "It seemed like a pretty big deal to me."

Her frustrated confusion dissolved. "I love you too."

Theo lifted his eyebrows. "You do?"

"Yes! I thought it was obvious."

"It is, but we haven't said it out loud, and when Marco opened his big mouth, I thought you might misunderstand my silence."

It made sense—if they lived in a world of miscommunication and poor self-esteem. "Theo, I fell a little in love the first—second time I saw you."

"Me too." He kissed her, wrapped his arms around her, and swung her around.

After he brought her back down to earth, Allie said, "I don't want to assume anything, but just for future reference, if you should ever have something really important along these lines to say, would you please do it quickly? This just about killed me."

He laughed. "I can't imagine what you could be talking about, but I will keep that in mind."

Arm in arm, they headed inside, feeling a bit more sure-footed.

They were almost at the door when Dylan strode past them. "Good night."

Despite their stunned curiosity, they each

managed to turn before footsteps approached from the other direction.

Allie said quietly, "Let me talk to her."

With a knowing nod, Theo slipped discretely inside.

"Eve?"

Eve's voice wavered. "Allie, thanks for everything. I've got to go."

"Why don't I get us a couple of hot coffee drinks?" She leaned closer. "I'm in pretty good with the owner. I bet I can get him to throw in an extra shot of something." She slipped her arm into Eve's and led her to the door. "We can sit by the wood stove. All the diners are gone, so that corner is empty. The pub crowd's too busy watching a game. They won't even know that we're there."

Eve didn't agree, but she didn't disagree, either, so Allie continued to lead her inside. After a brief detour to ask Theo for some drinks, they sat down by the fire.

Allie said, "It feels good by the fire. It's getting chilly outside. I guess it's inevitable. The seasons are changing."

"It's over with Dylan."

Allie took in a quick breath. She'd feared as much, but she hated to hear it.

"He and Jack always had issues in high school. They were friends, but Dylan was different. Of course, Jack was oblivious. He still is. I don't know why I didn't see that before. Well, yes, I do. He was everything I thought I could want in a guy—

athletic, extremely good-looking, and popular. Why did that seem so important back then?" Eve shook her head.

Theo arrived with two coffee drinks swirled with whipped cream on top. With those delivered, he gave Allie's shoulder a squeeze and went back to the bar.

Eve continued. "Dylan said he was always in Jack's shadow. He won't go there again. Seeing Jack sent him back to those days. Jack always got what he wanted. He still does, I imagine. His business looks very successful. He's a prominent member of the community. Some things never change." She leaned her head back against the rocking chair. "Except Dylan. He moved beyond the past years ago and refuses to go there again."

Allie couldn't find fault with Dylan. From what little she'd heard, he had every reason to put distance between himself and Jack. "And he thinks having Jack in your life will bring back those old high school dynamics?"

"Exactly." She paused, overwhelmed with emotion. "But Jack is Lydia's father, and she wants to know him. I didn't ask for him to come back into our lives, but Lydia did. I can't take him from her now."

Ally said, "I don't understand. Did Dylan give you an ultimatum?"

"Not exactly. He just can't do it, or he won't. I don't think he can help it." Eve sighed. "He told me he liked me back then, in high school. I never knew it. I barely knew him. He was Jack's friend, always in the periphery. I didn't know this till now, but back then, he told Jack that he liked me. Shortly after that, Jack suddenly noticed me, and he offered me a ride home from a party. Lydia was the result. I never told anyone, but Dylan figured it out, and he's always resented Jack for it. There's been bad blood between them ever since."

Allie wasn't sure what to say. "That's quite a burden to carry around all these years."

Eve nodded and took a sip of her drink. "I think that's why—along with us both being shy—it's been hard for us to let down our guard and be together. He was afraid to risk caring again, and I haven't trusted my heart since I gave it away to a guy who didn't notice or care. In spite of it all, we were building something. It was early, but it was something good."

"Oh, Eve."

"I'm in love with him, Allie."

She wasn't surprised. Her heart broke for Eve.

"My heart is his, but he just doesn't get it."

"Have you told him?"

"Not in so many words. I was waiting for the right time—maybe after he said it first."

"Don't you think, in his way, he has already shown you? He is head over heels crazy about you, and everyone sees it."

Eve couldn't believe what she was hearing. "I was hoping. I thought maybe, but... really?"

Allie nodded, confirming. "He loves you, and you love him too."

Tears came to Eve's eyes as she nodded.

"Before you give up, don't you think you should tell him you love him?"

"It's too late. Maybe it's for the best. My life used to be simple and secure. But this is like a roller coaster ride that's too scary to stay on, except you're stuck on it until it's over—which I guess it is now."

"I refuse to believe that."

Eve smiled sadly. "There was a window in time when it might have worked out, but that window is closed."

"No," Allie said resolutely. "No, I'm calling an emergency lunch meeting. We're all going to put our heads together and get this train back on track."

Eve managed a weak smile. "You're so sweet, but some things can't be fixed."

Allie's eyes brightened as she cleared her throat. "Excuse me, but have you forgotten who you're dealing with here? We could rule the world from that lunch group. In fact, I should bring that up at the next meeting." She gave Eve her best no-nonsense look. "We will work this out." She topped it off with a confident nod.

# CHAPTER SIXTEEN

Late at night, Lydia sat up in bed, unable to sleep. She glanced over at the window and recalled how Marco had climbed through it to rescue her—even though she hadn't needed it. But it made her feel good that he cared. No other guy had climbed up a tree to her window.

She picked up her phone and texted him. *Are you awake?*

Marco: *Yeah, me and everyone else around here. Your mother and Dylan left a while ago. I'm surprised she's not home by now.*

Lydia: *Oh, she's home. That's not why I texted.*

Marco: ???

Lydia: *I can't sleep.*

Marco: *I told you, switch to decaf. You're wound up pretty tight.*

Lydia: *Thanks, Dr. Phil. I wish it were that easy.*

Marco: *Okay. What is it, my child?*

Lydia: *Well, Father Marco (???), I've ruined my mother's life.*

Marco: *Wow. Her whole life? That's some superpower you've got there. Don't tell your mom. She might ground you.*

Lydia: *This is me not laughing.*

Marco: *Sorry. What's wrong?*

Lydia: *My dad came to see me.*

Marco: *Really?! That's huge!*

Lydia: *Yeah, and so was the fight my mom had with Dylan.*

Marco: *Oh.*

Lydia: *Exactly. Now they've broken up.*

Marco: *Why? Dylan had to have known you had a father somewhere. I mean, I think that's how it works, right?*

Lydia: *Oh, it is. And apparently Dylan was best friends with Jack. When my mother got pregnant, Dylan proposed to her!*

Marco: *Wow! And you know this because...?*

Lydia: *I'm a good listener?*

Marco: *Wait. That night I climbed into your window... you knew then?*

Lydia: *Yeah, I thought I told you.*

Marco: *Uh. No. You just told me about Jack.*

Lydia: *Oh. Well, I had a lot on my mind.*

Marco: *But I don't get it. They broke up because...?*

Lydia: *Short version, Mom had to choose between Dylan or Jack.*

Marco: *Wait. She and Jack are a thing now?*

Lydia: *No! Dylan hates Jack, so if Jack's in our lives (as my father—not her boyfriend), Dylan's out.*

Marco: *Oh, that sucks. But how is that your fault?*

Lydia: *Come on, Marco. Keep up. If I hadn't gone to see Jack, none of this would have happened. My mother and Dylan would still be crazy in love, and I wouldn't feel like a big steamy pile of poop.*

Marco: *Watch your language there, missy. :D*

Lydia: *I'm serious!*

Marco: *So am I. Sometimes.*

Lydia lowered her phone to her lap and stared at the wall. "I've got to go see him." Her phone chimed.

Marco: *Hello?*

Lydia: *I know what to do now. Thanks!*

Marco: *You're welcome. For what?*

Lydia: *I've got to see Dylan.*

Marco: *Tonight? It's past midnight.*

Lydia: *Not now. Tomorrow.*

Marco: *Oh. You mean after classes?*

Lydia: *I guess.*

Marco: *Good idea. Uh... Lydia?*

Lydia: *Yes?*

Marco: *How were you planning to get there?*

Lydia: *Oh.*

Marco: *I'll take you there after class.*

Lydia: *Really? THANK YOU!!!*

Marco: *Calm down. It's only a ride.*

Lydia: (*thank you*)

MARCO PARKED the truck in front of Vaughan Plumbing, which housed the business in back and a house in front, where Dylan lived with his parents.

Marco said, "I'll go grab something to eat. Don't worry. I'll bring something back for you. If you need me, I've got my phone here."

Lydia hesitated before getting out of the car. "You know, you're a really good friend."

"I've never had a friend who's a girl," Marco said.

"Don't worry. I don't think you've broken any laws of nature."

He flashed that smile that charmed all the girls. "I know. It's just... different."

Lydia didn't know how to react. "Glad I could help."

"Help with what?"

"I don't know. I was just thinking it might be kind of lonely there as the only caveman in the twenty-first century."

He laughed. "A caveman with a car. You can't argue with that."

She grew serious. "No, I can't. What would I do without you?"

"A lot of walking." He grinned. "Go on. I'll be waiting."

Lydia walked up to Dylan's front door and rang the doorbell.

Dylan opened the door and, after registering some initial surprise, gave her a kind smile. "Lydia."

"Can we talk? It's important."

"Come on in."

A voice called out from the kitchen, "Who was that?"

Dylan leaned closer and said quietly, "It's my dad. Hold on." He was halfway to the kitchen door when his father appeared in the doorway. Not quite as tall as Dylan, with thinning gray hair, he had the same amiable manner as Dylan.

Dylan said, "Dad, this is Lydia, Eve's daughter."

"Lydia! We've met, but you wouldn't remember." He grinned. "Have you eaten? I was just making a sandwich."

"No, thanks, Mr. Vaughan. I just stopped by for a quick word with Dylan."

"Okay. If you change your mind, let us know."

"I will. Thank you."

Owen Vaughan's eyes crinkled as he smiled. "All right, then. I've got some sliced deli ham calling my name."

When he was gone, Dylan said, "Let's go sit on the porch."

The porch was closed in with large windows on three sides. It was chilly but more private than the living room would have been. Once seated, Dylan wasted no time. "What's on your mind?"

Lydia searched for the words. No matter how many conversations she had rehearsed in her head on the way over, she still wasn't sure what to say. "When I went to see Jack—"

That was as far as Dylan let her get. "I don't want to talk about Jack."

"I know, but I need to."

Dylan exhaled. "I know you mean well—"

Lydia blurted out, "It's my fault. It's all my fault. You and my mom were so happy, and then I had to go look for Jack. I never meant to hurt anybody."

"Don't blame yourself. You did nothing wrong."

Lydia had wanted more than anything not to be emotional, but even though she kept it inside, she still couldn't think clearly. "I just wanted to see him. After all, he's my father. And he made an effort to see me."

Dylan muttered, "After eighteen years."

"But he did come to see me, and that's worth something."

Dylan stared at the ground.

"And besides, what kind of a person would I be if I couldn't forgive him?"

"Normal." Dylan leaned back as though being patient took everything out of him.

"I don't know what's going to come of it."

Dylan said softly, "I have a pretty good idea."

"I know, and you're probably right. But he's my father, and I want to know him. Is that so strange?"

"No, and your mother won't stand in your way. She's a remarkable woman."

"I know—and she deserves to be happy. Dylan, you make her happy. I've never seen her like she is with you. I know it can't have been easy for her to raise me alone. She's never complained, but I know I was a burden."

"Children aren't a burden. They're a blessing."

Lydia smiled. "An annoying blessing, in my case, I'm sure."

Dylan laughed. "We all have our moments, but she can be very proud of the young woman you've become."

"I think—I hope she's proud. But now it's her turn. She deserves a chance to be happy." Lydia leaned toward him. "You are that chance. If Mom loses you, I will never forgive myself."

"Ah, here it is—the guilt card."

Lydia shook her head. It was not going well.

Dylan's eyes softened. "I get it. He's your father. Blood is thicker than water. I do understand." He leaned his elbows on his knees. "I want what's best for your mother and for you. But that doesn't mean I can like it or want to be around it—around Jack."

"It's not like they'll be a couple. He'll just be around now and then."

"I'm sorry, but I just can't do it." Dylan stood.

Lydia wished she had asked Marco to wait. Just then, he pulled up in front of the house. Wishing she could say something to change Dylan's mind, she looked at him, but it was no use. "Bye, Dylan."

# CHAPTER SEVENTEEN

On the outskirts of Pine Harbor, a heavy rain fell, meeting patches of fog drifting up from the water. In its midst, a small café seemed suspended in air from its precarious perch on the rocks that sloped sharply down to the water. At the end of a Friday workday, most people bypassed it in favor of the bar down the road, and that made the café perfect for this particular event.

The last to arrive, Allie dashed from her car to the awning that jutted out from the entrance. Shaking her umbrella vigorously, she stomped her feet for good measure and walked inside. At the opposite end of the entrance, Caroline, Kim, and Lydia waved.

Once Allie was settled, Kim struck her spoon on the table like a gavel. "I hereby call to order this emergency meeting of the Pine Harbor Lunch—you know, we really need a better name for it—Club."

With a patient smile for Kim, Allie said, "First order of business: I think we all agree that those two need help." Everyone knew that by "those two," she meant Eve and Dylan.

Caroline was just coming off a busy work week, so she regarded Lydia with a questioning look. "So, Eve and Dylan had a falling out, obviously. I work with the woman. She's been miserable all week, but she won't talk."

"They broke up," Lydia said, "but she loves him."

Allie nodded in absolute agreement. "Theo refuses to get involved, but I've managed to squeeze some covert intelligence out of him. Based on his conversations with Dylan, he loves her too."

Kim said, "Just to clarify, you're talking about Dylan."

Annoyed, Allie wrinkled her face. "Yes, Dylan. Theo doesn't love Eve. He loves me!"

Kim's face lit up. "Aha! So he's actually said it! He loves you!"

Allie blushed as she confessed. "Yes."

Kim lifted her coffee cup. "Well, hear! Hear!"

After clinking coffee cups together, Allie said, "Let's get back to the agenda."

Kim's ears perked up. "Agenda? What agenda? I didn't get one."

Caroline's eyes twinkled as she proceeded. "Back to Eve and Dylan. We've got two people in love, so that's good. The only thing in the way is

Jack. By the way, who's Jack, and why is he in the way?"

Kim nodded. "Yeah, I think I missed that part too."

Allie explained, "That's what the whole firepit incident was about."

"I still don't understand," Caroline said.

Allie and Lydia exchanged looks, then Lydia said, "This can't go past this group."

Kim's eyes widened. "Oh, this group has a strict code of confidence."

Caroline smiled at Kim's histrionics. "Seriously, I don't recall any leaks from this group."

Lydia took a deep breath. "Jack's my father."

A long stretch of wide eyes and stunned silence followed, then Lydia added, "Dylan hates Jack." No one asked why, but the curiosity was easy to see on their faces, so Lydia did her best to briefly recap the story.

Caroline's eyes softened as she regarded Lydia. "What exactly does Jack want?"

"I think he just wants to get to know me, and I want that too."

Kim's eyebrows appeared stuck together as she said, "But Dylan's jealous. Does he need to be?"

"No!" Lydia looked shocked at the very suggestion.

Kim added, "Just clarifying."

Always the logical one, Caroline summed it up. "So, worst-case scenario, Jack stops by now and then to see you. He's not interested in rebuilding a family together."

"No! He's got his own life. We've got ours. But now I've got a dad. I don't think my mom wants any more to do with him than she has to. She's just doing this for me."

All of this confirmed Allie's understanding. "I can't help but think that if Dylan could somehow get used to the idea, he and Eve could work through this."

Kim nodded, thinking. "We need to get them together."

The others exchanged looks upon hearing the obvious stated as if it were a revelation. Seeing them, Kim explained, "What I mean is, we need to get them together so Dylan can view Eve through a love haze."

Almost in unison, the others asked, "A love haze?"

Kim shrugged. "What? You know what I mean. You're in love. You look at that special someone, and you see them through a magical haze." She pointed at the window and the rainy weather outside. "Kinda like that fog rolling in, but with a smokin' hot guy in the middle of it."

"Okay..." Allie said, more from politeness than from agreement.

There was no stopping Kim now. She unfolded her plan with a good deal of dramatic gesturing. "We need some kind of romantic situation. Except they won't just show up if they know the other one's gonna be there, so we need to surprise them with love."

Allie watched in astonishment. For all of Kim's quirky individuality, that creative mind of hers was a thing to behold.

Kim said, "If he suddenly sees her, he'll be caught off guard, and he'll remember how desperately he loves her." Her dreamlike tone changed to a practical one. "That's where the love haze comes in. There's no fighting it once that fog rolls in, clouding his emotions and eyes. At that point, he'll just want to find a way through it."

Lydia squinted. "Find a way through the fog?"

"No," Kim said. "Through the roadblock." Met with blank stares, she added, "Jack."

Caroline leaned back. "You know, that could work."

Kim looked a little offended. "You don't have to look so surprised."

Allie laughed. "Okay, so we all agree." Everyone nodded. "We need to find some way to ambush them."

Kim's eyebrows drew together. "'Ambush' is such a strong word."

Allie finished her coffee and stared at the saucer. "But how?"

Kim shrugged. "I don't know. Give me a minute. It can't be that hard. This isn't rocket science."

"No, it's worse." Caroline set down her coffee. "There's no logic involved."

"Oh, Caroline," Kim said sweetly. "You can't logic your way into love."

Allie caught Lydia's eye, and they both suppressed laughter.

Without warning, Kim slammed her palm on the table, and everyone flinched. "I've got it!" She threw her palms up as though a crowd were cheering her for her brilliance. "A costume party!"

Caroline lifted her eyebrows. "Kim, you amaze me."

"You're welcome." She pulled a pen from her purse, grabbed a napkin, and jotted down notes. "So, let's hammer out some details, ladies."

# CHAPTER EIGHTEEN

A WEEK LATER, it was the Saturday before Halloween and the night of their costume party. Theo couldn't leave the bar, so they'd brought the party to him. He advertised it as a costume night, but the costume had to fully disguise the person wearing it—a key component of Kim's plan.

Dressed as a bottle of a Silva Brothers' craft beer, Marco was manning the music when Kim approached him. "Hey, Cinderella!"

"Kimberella," she corrected him as she pulled him aside then explained his part of the plan to him.

Lydia approached Kim, but before she could speak, Kim said, "You know that you're wearing the same costume as Marco, right?"

"Oh, I know. We're a six pack of Silva Brothers' beer—Marco, Theo, Allie, Caroline, Mel, and me. That's our carton over there in the corner. That lasted two minutes—long enough to post a picture online. So, what if this dance doesn't work?"

"It'll work. It worked in *West Side Story*."

"But they were trained dancers."

"You don't need to be trained for this. Trust me."

"What if they don't want to dance?"

"Oh, they'll dance! Caroline is shadowing Eve, and Allie's in charge of Dylan. It's happening."

"Are they here?"

"Yeah, somewhere. If you see a recently declassified alien, that's Eve. And—oh, there he is. See Bigfoot? That's Dylan."

"They'll make a cute couple."

Kim made a face. "The inventory was kind of low at the costume shop." She grabbed a mic and announced that they were starting the evening with a dance. "Boys on the outside, girls on the inside." With some coaxing from Kim, almost two dozen people got into place. She continued. "When the music stops, you stop. When the music starts up again, dance like nobody's watching with your new partner. The first couple to guess each other's names gets a drink on the house."

After making sure Marco chose something slow, Kim gave him the signal to start the music, then he stopped right on cue. Alien Eve and Bigfoot Dylan were partnered. Kim could hardly contain her joy at her success. Allie and Caroline joined Kim, who was beaming. It was going so well until a giant banana tripped on its peel and knocked Eve over, sending her alien mask flying. Marco stopped the music while Eve lay stunned.

FORGETTING ANY PROBLEMS THEY HAD, Dylan knelt down to Eve. "Are you okay?"

She looked up at Bigfoot. "I think so." She started to stand.

Bigfoot helped her to her feet, and the music resumed. He led her to a table in the corner and sat across from her. "Are you sure you're okay?"

"What?"

He said it again.

"Sorry. I can't understand you through the fur."

He pulled off his mask and repeated, "Are you sure you're okay?"

"Dylan." Between the fall and the mask, bits of Eve's hair were left pointing in different directions. Without thinking, Dylan reached out and smoothed her hair. It wasn't as if he hadn't missed her. His heart ached constantly. But he kept thinking of how much it would ache when Jack stole her heart again. But as he looked at her gentle eyes and soft lips, he remembered her kiss. All he could think of was sweeping her into his arms and kissing those lips again. Resisting was torture.

Eve asked, "How are you?"

*How am I?* He wanted to cry out the answer. *I miss you! How could you even ask?* "I'm fine."

"Good."

Dylan nodded. When their eyes met, it felt like a blow to the gut, but he couldn't look away. Then his guarded emotions broke free. "We keep finding ourselves in the right place, but the time's always wrong. Eve, I'm sorry." He couldn't look at those soft round eyes anymore. Somehow, he found the strength to stand and leave.

"Wait!"

He turned.

Eve stood and lifted her chin. "I have something to say."

He couldn't bear the silence that followed. "Eve." He glanced toward the door.

She grabbed his arm. "Don't go."

"Eve, it's too late. We've been over this."

Anger burned in her eyes. "No, *you've* been over this! But, Dylan, I love you!"

"No."

"Do you think you're the only one who can love?"

Her anger sparked his own. "Don't tell me about love. I have loved you since high school. I loved you while Jack was breaking your heart. I loved you before Lydia was born, and I've loved you all the eighteen years since. So don't lecture me about love!"

"Then why can't we—"

"Jack. He will bring nothing but pain, and I won't be a part of it anymore."

"Jack can go take a flying... ride in his pumpkin balloon!"

Dylan couldn't seem to make himself leave.

"And so can you." She walked away but turned back. "No!" She drew in a breath. "For years, I have tried to ignore my true feelings because they once betrayed me. I came to believe I was better off feeling safe—even if that meant being alone." She looked at him, and that look broke his heart. "I don't want to be safe anymore. I just want to be with you."

Dylan closed the space between them so quickly, he heard a soft gasp as he pulled her against him. "I'll keep you safe." If one kiss could hold a lifetime of passion, theirs did.

As if out of nowhere, Eve's friends appeared nearby in a clump. Kim held up part of a plant. "It's a pumpkin vine. I'd like to think it's kind of a Halloween version of mistletoe. Apparently, you two don't need it, so..." She stretched it over the top of her head. "I wonder if I could make a headband out of this."

# CHAPTER NINETEEN

Light snow drifted silently down upon Caroline's home, gently dusting the roof and the pine trees. The Saturday before Thanksgiving had given over to winter as Eve and her tight-knit group of friends gathered for a Friendsgiving dinner. Caroline sent Kim from the kitchen with hors d'oeuvres, then Kim made a detour to check out the Notre Dame football game on TV.

Dylan snuck up behind Eve. "Let me help you with that." Then he put his arms around her and took over tossing the salad while he whispered in her ear. A blush rose to her cheeks as a soft smile brought a glow to her eyes. Glancing over her shoulder, she whispered, "I can't work like this."

"Daddy!" With an eye roll for her father, Hailey reached for the salad tongs. "Here, Eve, let me help."

"Thanks, Hailey, but I've got a better idea. Let's put your father to work."

With a grin, Hailey offered the salad tongs to her father. "Your turn, Daddy. Eve and I will supervise you."

"Oh, you two are a dangerous pair."

Eve winked at Hailey as they watched Dylan at work.

In the hallway, Theo cornered Allie and stole a kiss just as Marco and Lydia happened along. Marco covered Lydia's eyes. "Hey, you two! Not in front of the children!" While he ushered Lydia past the hallway, she broke free and swatted his arm. "Who are you calling children?"

Laughing and ducking, he said, "Sorry. Child."

Caroline gathered them all around the buffet and said a blessing. Just as she finished and Marco took a step toward the food, Dylan said loudly, "Wait!"

Everyone stopped.

"I've got a little announcement. Well, it's a big announcement, actually."

"Does it involve food?" Kim asked. "'Cause I'm starving!"

Dylan cast a nervous look in her direction. "You're not making this any easier."

Eve took pity on him and blurted out, "We're engaged!"

"What?" Kim cried. "That was quick!"

Dylan glanced at Eve with a glint in his eyes. "Yeah, nineteen years, and she's already agreed to marry me."

Kim lifted her arms in the air. "Well, thank

God!" Then she looked around at all the eyes fixed on her. "What? It's Thanksgiving, and I'm giving thanks."

Dylan put one arm around his daughter and the other around Eve. "So am I."

Don't miss the next book in the Pine Harbor series:

*Being best friends was perfect—until she fell in love.*
Lydia's Pine Harbor Christmas

# THE PINE HARBOR TRILOGY

Join the women of Pine Harbor, Maine on their delightful journey of love, friendship, and surprises

Life is full of unexpected moments. For three close-knit friends, a viral proposal, a long-awaited second chance, and a friendship that blossoms into love will change everything. Follow their messy, heartwarming, and hilarious quests to navigate past wounds and modern chaos to find their happily ever afters. This sweet and uplifting contemporary romance trilogy celebrates the power of hope, humor, and the courage to choose love against all odds. Perfect for readers who want to laugh, swoon, and have their hearts warmed.

jljarvis.com/pine-harbor/

# THANK YOU!

Thank you for reading! If you enjoyed this book, please consider leaving a review or a rating. Your feedback on bookstore, Goodreads, and Bookbub websites helps other readers discover books they'll enjoy.

## ALSO BY J.L. JARVIS

**Waterfront Summers**

(Can be read in any order)

*The Cottage at Peregrine Cove*

*The House on Serenity Lake*

*Moonlight on Mariner's Bluff*

**Drake & Wilde Mysteries**

(Reading Order)

1 *Love in the Time of Pumpkins*

2 *Secrets in the Hollow*

3 *Shadow of the Horseman*

**Standalones**

(Can be read in any order)

*A Cowboy Kind of Love*

*A Christmas Eve Stop*

*Christmas by Lamplight*

*A Kiss in the Rain*

*App-ily Ever After*

*Once Upon a Winter*

*The Red Rose*

*Highland Vow*

## Short Stories

(Can be read in any order)

*The Magic of Snow*

*The Eleventh-Hour Pact*

*A Christmas Yarn*

*The Farmer and the Belle*

*Work-Crush Balance*

## Cedar Creek

(Can be read in any order)

*Christmas at Cedar Creek*

*Snowstorm at Cedar Creek*

*Sunlight on Cedar Creek*

## Pine Harbor

1 *Allison's Pine Harbor Summer*

2 *Evelyn's Pine Harbor Autumn*

3 *Lydia's Pine Harbor Christmas*

## Holiday House

(Can be read in any order)

*The Christmas Cabin*

*The Winter Lodge*

*The Lighthouse*

*The Christmas Castle*

*The Beach House*

*The Christmas Tree Inn*

*The Holiday Hideaway*

## Highland Passage

(Can be read in any order)

*Highland Passage*

*Knight Errant*

*Lost Bride*

## Highland Soldiers

1 *The Enemy*

2 *The Betrayal*

3 *The Return*

4 *The Wanderer*

## American Hearts

(Can be read in any order)

*Secret Hearts*

*Forbidden Hearts*

*Runaway Hearts*

For more information, visit jljarvis.com.

Get monthly book news at news.jljarvis.com.

# ABOUT THE AUTHOR

J.L. Jarvis is a left-handed former opera singer/teacher/lawyer who writes books. She now lives and writes on a mountaintop in upstate New York.

jljarvis.com

instagram.com/jljarvis.writer
facebook.com/jljarvis1writer
x.com/JLJarvis_writer
youtube.com/@jljarvis-author
bookbub.com/authors/j-l-jarvis

www.ingramcontent.com/pod-product-compliance
Lightning Source LLC
Chambersburg PA
CBHW050843180626
46814CB00007B/2603
* 9 7 8 1 9 4 2 7 6 7 3 7 4 *